Larwock

Sam Zadgan

Contents

A town called Larwock

I.   A strange night

Some places exist and don't exist all at the same time; the people wonder in and out of our realms freely. But what would it take for normal folk, from normal cities, living normal lives to somehow stumble into these opaque worlds? A wrong turn down a road that exists only for the alluring purpose of drawing innocence, a bait to tempt unforgiving fate, could be such a way.

A newly married couple driving cross-country to a holiday destination could be the beginning. Before modern technology and GPS systems existed, a simpler time of maps, the couple stumbles upon such a T-junction.

Tamara couldn't find this particular spot on the map, and shrugged, but this surely was her mistake—as was the last time they lost their way, over two hours ago. James brought the car to a standstill and retrieved the map. He followed the path they had taken with an eagle-eyed focus, but after a short moment lifted his head and looked around, peering through each window of their sedan.

He stepped outside the car with the map. It was a sunny day, approximately four in the afternoon, and the sun was making its way to the west where the amber glow was still above the mountains. The road was nestled between dense trees and bush with the eastern side dropping down into a valley below—not steep or threatening, but a vista of natural beauty of rivers and fauna. The junction ahead had no signs and James referred back to his map, unravelling it in its entirety on the hood of the car. He inspected it from the last check point. There was only one road they could have taken: the road they were on. This should have led them to the next town for a night's rest before their next day of driving to Melbourne. They planned a week of honeymooning in the city before they had to come back and resume life as a wedded couple.

The map was not providing any assistance. He looked to his left at the sun, setting to the west, so he walked towards the junction to peer down each path. He noticed that to the left, the road seemed to turn in a southern direction, whereas the road on the right continued straight for as far as he could see.

James went back in the car, folded the map and handed it back to Tamara, his hunch was to turn left. The plan was, if within thirty minutes they were not in the town, they would turn back and try the other direction. The map would suggest that they were very close to their town of Bowral anyway. Driving down the road they noticed a few pedestrians walking on the side of the road, bearing backpacks and dressed for a day of hiking—this gave the young couple confidence that they were heading in the right direction. Shortly, the trees disappeared and gave way to the view up ahead. There was a small stream with a single lane bridge, from which they could see a few houses and shops in the distance. The bridge was narrow and they had to wait while an oncoming car crossed before them.

The town was quiet and the stores were closing, but they were yet to see the hotel they would be staying at for the night. They did, however, see a small and well maintained motel, which James drove towards. Parking, James left Tamara in the car as he enquired about the hotel and town. He came back to the car sheepishly.

"We're not in Bowral, it was the other direction." James spoke apologetically as Tamara sighed and rolled her eyes. "But he said that the road into town turns back onto the main road after Bowral and we're no worse off."

Tamara didn't seem to see the positive side.

"He's offering us a room, but there's no one staying tonight, so he'll give us the deluxe suite for the price of a normal room. What do you think?" James waited for an answer.

Tamara thought for a moment "But what about the other hotel we booked?" she shot back.

"It's okay, we didn't pay anything. I'll call them to tell them what's happened. To be honest, I'd prefer to just stay the night here and go tomorrow morning rather than driving another hour to Bowral."

Tamara finally nodded in agreement.

The logic was fair and the town looked nice and quaint— in addition, the deluxe suite sounded like an appealing offer. James started to unload the car as Tamara walked into the motel and completed the dated paper work, which involved a name, address and a $15 deposit for the night. She collected the key and with James they walked up the stairs to the first floor, which evidently was the top floor with two rooms.

The Elder Inn was the second building to be erected in the town of Larwock. It had been standing for a hundred years, per the plaque next to the room door. By the sounds of the creaking floor boards under their feet it was easy to fathom the age of the building. Upon entering the room they were hit with a stale and musky odour and James was quick to open the windows.

Later that night, James and Tamara settled into a deep sleep after a day of driving with little rest, but it was short lived as an inhumane scream echoed throughout the streets and into their room. The couple sobered from sleep instantly and James rushed to the window. Below he witnessed a scene that only appeared in nightmares. There was a small crowd of fifty or so people, walking in double line formation through the street, being led by one red-haired woman dressed in a white robe.

Halfway down the line he noticed a naked woman being held up above the participants' heads. She screamed again, but there was no sign of struggle. The sound was enough to prompt Tamara to the window, just as James noticed the red-haired woman staring right into his eyes.

For a moment her deathly stare instilled fear into his very bones, but then she smiled at him and turned back as the line continued to walk through the town. James shut the window and closed the curtains, and they both sat nervously in their bed.

A moment passed and it was quiet again, but the silence broke with a creaking in the floor boards and footsteps from the stairs. The footsteps became lighter as they approached the landing and only the creaking floorboards under foot could be heard, getting closer to the deluxe suite door. James looked around the bed, and then at the fireplace. He leaped across the bed and retrieved the fire log poker; it was heavy, sharp and reassuringly well built. He stood by the door as the footsteps ceased. James and Tamara exchanged a look—were they overreacting?

Then the blind noises they heard affirmed their reactions. First, a rolling of keys on a keyring, shuffling to find the right one. James raised the poker, taking a deep breath. Next, the key was inserted, clicking each rivet into place, and the door knob slowly turned as Tamara curled in fear.

The door knob turned clockwise and hit the end of the turn, but to no avail; it turned faster this time anti-clockwise and hit the end of the turn, but again the door did not open. Then the doorknob violently shook from one direction to the other. There was another haunting scream from the demonic parade outside. Altogether it pushed Tamara over the edge, the fear too much to contain, and she shook uncontrollably and then screamed!

At that instant, everything stopped, there was silence again and Tamara was in tears and shivering involuntarily.

James stepped closer to the door and motioned to Tamara to remain calm as he opened the door, poker in hand and ready to swing at whatever stood outside. But he was met by a low-lit barren corridor, with no signs of anyone or anything being present. James was ready to leave the inn that night, until he heard the most comforting sound of the night. From next door, the sound of the key turning the lock, and footsteps walking deeper into the room and disappearing.

James put down the poker and comforted Tamara on the bed. This was a strange night, and they would leave, but it seemed less sinister than a moment ago. Holding each other close and safe, they reluctantly turned in for a light sleep till the morning.

2.   A plausible explanation

Usually the morning call of a rooster, for better or worse, woke those within hearing distance and signalled the start to the day. For James and Tamara, however, it was a call that was welcomed, not for ending a sombre sleep, but a signal that they could leave this place and forget the horrid night before.

The young couple was already packed and ready to leave as they opened their door to head down the stairs. But upon reaching the front desk, James was stunned to see the old man with the red-haired woman from the parade the night before talking quietly in the foyer. His hopes of leaving unnoticed were dashed as the red-haired woman turned to him with a sweet smile and apologetic eyes.

"Oh my, we are so sorry. I've just been talking to Harold here and he told me he heard a scream from your room last night. Did we scare you with our little parade?"

James was surprised with the tone and nature of the red-haired woman and he was ushered into a state of calm. He put the bags down for a moment.

"It wasn't just that, there was someone at our door trying to get in. We are leaving anyway, so…" James said as he reached down to his bags, but Harold interrupted him.

"That was your bloody neighbour. Steve does that all the time—he gets blind drunk and doesn't know his arse from his elbow." He apologetically continued, "Like the good lady says, we are sorry, mate, and I'm not going to charge you any money for your night's stay."

James for a moment questioned his reaction and wild thoughts from the previous night. He started to feel a little guilty as Tamara walked past him towards the car. But she had no time for guilt or explanations, she wanted to leave and forget the events of the night. After a few steps out of the inn, Tamara was frozen in her tracks. She was met with a horrid sight.

"JAMES!" she screamed. All three turned to her in slight shock. "They've slit our tyres! What the hell is going on here?"

Tamara was overcome with feelings of helplessness, and the coincidental sequences of occurrences so far were too heavy for her shoulders. James, dismayed, walked past Tamara and rushed outside to inspect for himself. She was right. James stood for a moment looking around the town, which was already buzzing with a small number of people going into the shops and going about their daily errands.

Harold and the red-haired woman left the inn and stood at the door with Tamara, inspecting the car, while James was beyond words.

"Bloody hell, mate, that's shit. You wait 'ere, I'll give Johnny a call and see if he can fix it up for ya… Bloody hell." Harold's tone and concern seemed genuine enough.

With that, Harold walked back into the inn, leaving the

three staring at the car. James turned to the red-haired woman with anger and frustration.

"What are you people playing at?" James shot the words out like daggers. She glanced at Tamara for any support against her partner, but there was no remorse in Tamara either.

"What on earth do you mean?" she defended, before James stepped menacingly closer.

"I mean, that shit last night and now this… If this is not fixed I'm going to phone the police and…" Before he had a chance to finish that threat, Harold exited the inn with good news.

Harold had spoken to Johnny, the local mechanic, and he was bringing his truck to tow the car back to his workshop and replace the tyres. This welcoming news seemed to take James and Tamara off the knife's edge and the mood settled slightly. The red-haired woman took the opportunity to talk with a less hostile audience.

"I'm sorry if our ways are somewhat backwards for city folk like you, but last night was our hundred-year celebrations. It was a harmless re-enactment of our founders' escape and discovery of Larwock. Every twenty-five years we have a three-day celebration and last night was the first night." She stepped past James and got a closer look at the tyres. "As for your car, I can only hazard a guess to say that a bunch of overzealous teenage boys vandalised it. I can assure you, there is nothing more sinister or cerebral than that."

The explanation, both plausible and logical, fell together in a coherent account of exactly what took place the night before, and the young couple began feeling embarrassed and ashamed of the conclusions they had drawn from the events. Defeated and humbled, James and Tamara apologised, to which they received an equally genuine forgiveness and were directed to the local café to have breakfast whilst their car was repaired.

Across the road, three shops south, stood Sammy's Milkbar, the local diner and coffee shop. Upon entry they were greeted by the owner, Sammy, wearing a white apron, white shirt and black tie, all freshly clean and pressed. James instantly recognised Sammy from the parade the night before; his distinctly shaped black beard was short and outlined his jawbone with no moustache and his balding head covering only the sides and back. He welcomed them warmly and showed them over to a booth by the window, with a clear view of the Elder Inn. After a few minutes Sammy returned with fresh coffee and two breakfast plates of eggs, bacon, sausages and toast.

"It's on the house. I heard what you people went through last night. I can imagine that would have been quite harrowing for tourists to witness."

Tamara couldn't contain her curiosity, however; especially now that she had been met with such hospitality since the events.

"What was that last night? Why was the girl screaming like that?" Tamara was genuinely interested as she took a sip of her coffee.

Sammy smiled, and then pulled out a chair from a nearby table and sat down next to the couple's booth.

"You see, that was our first night of celebrations. This town was founded a hundred years ago this week, and we do this parade every twenty-five years and re-enact our founders' escape from Bowral to Larwock. It's a lot of abracadabra…a lot of mumbo jumbo, but it's all good fun. The story goes…there was a coven of witches led by a wealthy man who were causing all types of havoc in Bowral. Some say they were getting ready to open the gates of hell or some rubbish like that. If you want my opinion, they were just a bunch of rich folk with too much cannabis!

"But anyway, the people of Bowral wanted no part of it, so one night the villagers put a stop to it. They ambushed the group and the group ran through the forest to this place. The villagers didn't follow them because they thought the forest was haunted and this group of witches had some power over it, or some such stuff… You want my opinion, they just wanted to get a bunch of drug addicts out of their town. I'm not even sure if I believe the whole story."

Sammy sensed that they were both taken by the story, so he continued with the tale as James and Tamara began eating their food.

"Anyway, this group ends up deciding to stay in the forest, so they start to cut down some trees and start building houses. The head of the coven's house is that there Elder Inn. The other building was the church. The whole group stayed in his house for a year and over that year they safeguarded the town from outsiders.

"They supposedly raised all types of demons and spirits to take ownership of the forest and protect them .. If you ask me, they just wanted to have orgies all the time in that house, but at some point they ran out of drugs and realised they needed their own places!"

"So, if they were devil worshippers, why did they build a church?" James looked a little puzzled as he posed the question.

"Well, they can still build a church…they just worship their own gods, and they weren't devil worshippers, they worshipped other gods, the Ancient Ones as they called it… something to do with old Persian sorcery or some rubbish, but very different, mate. In the end, like I said, all mumbo jumbo. I like the second and third night of celebrations anyway." He stopped as he looked out the window and noticed a person across the road.

"Oh…looks like Johnny's got some news for you." Sammy pointed to the man, Johnny, dressed in greasy blue overalls, heading to the café.

Johnny stepped inside the café nodding at Sammy, and then over to the couple's booth. With a sombre tone he apologetically told the couple the bad news.

"Sorry folks, I don't have those tyres in stock. I've just ordered a few from Sydney, and they'll be here tomorrow."

"Wait!" James shot back. "It's not that far to Sydney. One of us could be there and back within half a day, and anyway, Wollongong is like a half-hour drive."

"I tried Wollongong too," John dejectedly responded. "They are all out of stock. The guys in Sydney have to wait to get it from their distributors. If they order it now, they'll get it tomorrow morning and then they'll deliver it here by midday tomorrow. I'm sorry, that's the best I can do."

Johnny left the café as James and Tamara sat in their booth eating their breakfast and drinking their coffee, defeated and considering all the options left for them. But the lack of options was the most depressing thought of all. The idea of staying one more night in the town was not welcoming, but the hospitality of the residents had allayed some of their fears. Still there was a weird and uncommonness to this town that was unsettling to the couple; with hesitation, they agreed to stay another night.

Sammy approached the table, noticing the empty coffee cup.

"Let me fill that up for you…sorry, I overheard Johnny… so you guys staying the night?" James nodded in response. "Well, you should, it's going to be great. The celebrations tonight will be at the Elder Inn anyway, so you can join in."

James looked at Tamara, and they reluctantly nodded their heads.

"Great, it would be nice to have some new people at these things. You know a small town with the same people all the time can get really boring. New faces and new things to talk about…" Sammy was obviously enjoying the company of new faces.

"Oh hey, you know, if you're in town all day, you're welcome for lunch back here, but not on the house, I gotta make some money, right?" Sammy walked back to the counter, but before he got there he turned back. "Oh yeah, and while you're here you should look at our sights. The church is really nice, we don't use it, but it's nice to look around…and then there's the waterfall just outside of town, which has a really nice pool that some folk go swimming in…especially this time of year."

Sammy returned to the counter to serve coffee to the other customer, while the young couple looked out the window. There was nothing sinister, just people going about their business—the same people James saw the night before in the parade looked completely average now. The events of the night before could only be imagined in the deepest and darkest recesses of the mind, but today, a warm sun-filled day with no clouds, it all seemed a stretch of the imagination too far.

3. Exploring the town

After a short and restful nap, James and Tamara left their hotel room to explore the sights as Sammy suggested. Having secured a second night's stay at the Elder Inn, the young couple took their time in the room, starting with a long bath, all in an effort to turn a new leaf for the day. Upon leaving their room, the young newlyweds were startled by a man stumbling out of his room nextdoor: Steve, a burly man with a barrel chest, ginger hair, beard and green piercing eyes.

His attempt at external presentation was done well, but from the stench of alcohol emitting from his mouth it was obvious that internally he was still a mess. He grumbled and stumbled past the couple. He held onto the bannisters like a mountaineer negotiating a threatening climb as he struggled down the staircase. Tamara smiled at James; with one more mystery confirmed their stay in town seemed like a happy compromise.

Walking down the main street with the church on the southernmost part of the road, they walked past the entire town centre, passing shops of various nature. This was a small town, there were no department stores or supermarkets, and the isolation had kept the people appreciative of what they had and they were content with what they had, over the advances of neighbouring towns.

The sun was shining down strongly, but the awnings of the shops gave some relief as a cool breeze from the south seemed stronger in the shaded area and more noticeable. The young couple arrived at the steps of the church and were taken by the enormity of it, which wasn't evident before. Peering up at the structure, the size and height of it had magnified and looked ominous. The building "untouched for a hundred years" had managed to survive the pressures of age and environment and the wood panels although weathered on the surface were strong and solid beneath. The doors were open and dark shadows of statues could be seen from the entrance, which only served to entice the curiosity of the couple.

They climbed the steps onto the landing and immediately fell into a deep feeling of vertigo. The ground was flat but it felt as if they were walking on a warped floor with acute angles, which propelled their bodies into an unbalanced state. The angles seemed to change underfoot. They were absolutely bewildered when they looked down and saw only the flat ground, but lifting their heads they felt like they had boarded a boat in rough ocean waves, being swayed from side to side.

James griped Tamara's hand and was planning to jump back onto the street, when from behind a hand landed on his shoulder forcing them to take a step back, and everything settled down again.

"Are you folks okay? You seem like you were about to faint."

Tamara looked around to face an elderly man with a ragged shirt and dirty trousers. "Yes, everything is fine…

now…not sure what was going on for a second there," she responded gratefully.

"Oh, its okay, you folk just stumbled onto our Gateway Stone." He ushered the two into the church, both still shaken up by the Gateway Stone.

The old man took some time to elaborate on what they had just experienced.

"Yeah, that out there is what local folk call the Gateway Stone. Not sure if you know the history of this place, but one of the reasons they settled here a hundred years ago was because they thought the stone underneath that entrance to the church held special powers and was some kind of portal to another realm. No one can explain it, but when you stand on it, you feel like you're about to fall off the side of a ship."

James and Tamara sat down on the bench for moment to compose themselves as the old man told them about the stone. But once they regained their senses they couldn't help noticing the contents of the church instead. The old man's voice disappeared into silence as the vulgar shapes of statues came into focus.

The old man noticed their shift in focus. "Oh, don't let it get to you folks, these old statues are just statues,' he said reassuringly.

But Tamara looked up at the old man with a horrid gaze. "What kind of church is this? What are these statues?" she questioned.

The old man looked around at the five statues that stood in a circle in the middle of the church. He took a moment before explaining the best he could.

"I'm not the best person to ask, but they all represent an ancient god of an element: Fire, Water, Air, Earth and Spirit. They built these when they built the church. Mr Green, the head of the group that settled here, said that he'd seen these figures in his mind and communicated with them. They built the statues in honour of their protection of this town. I wouldn't read too much into it…just a bit of history, no one here believes this stuff anymore…but it's our history I guess."

Grotesque as the statues were, there was a fascination with something so unworldly and uncommon. A need for closer inspection was needed to witness the passion and madness that was required to carve out these life-size statues of malevolent features and shapes.

Tamara was first to approach the goat-looking creature at the head of the circle, representing Spirit. Its life-like hair was disturbing, but not as much as its eyes, which seemed to follow Tamara as she walked towards it, much like a Subirachs creation. The hair on the body and legs seemed like real goat hair to the touch, fresh and new as if living veins and organs were operating underneath. She also noticed a small slit on the left chest of the statue, as if something had been put inside via that hole and then been closed up to keep it in.

James on the other hand walked past the Fire element and towards the Water god: a serpentine creature with the slinky body of a snake and detailed scales in a series of diamond patterns on its back. But there were some discrepancies; firstly, the gills that bore resemblance to those of an eel, and a face so repugnant that it defied description.

A mixture of snake and human features in a manner that could only be imagined by an opium-induced madman.

As James floated closer, the statue became all too real. The forked tongue slightly protruded the human-like mouth and lips with sharp jagged teeth, seemingly glistening with saliva. He was drawn closer and closer yet, curiosity taking over. He stretched out his hand, attempting to touch the tongue and prove to himself it wasn't real. But a deep part of his consciousness was warning him, almost holding him back from touching it, the way a mouse feels when it's retrieving cheese from a trap.

A few sweat pebbles formed on his forehead the closer he got and those snake-like eyes locked in with his—under the serpent's charm he was drawn closer.

"Let's go, this place is giving me the creeps," Tamara said as she walked past James and startled him out of his trance-like state.

He composed himself and they left the church and the old man. Outside the church they headed further south, out of the town and towards the waterfall and natural pool. They found the trail quite easily, through some bush, a natural path made from years of townsfolk walking to and from the pool. They heard the sound of the waterfall in the distance behind some dense bushland.

They got to a clearing and beyond the rocks there was a small drop and they could see the waterfall, a small one, but pleasing to the eye as much of natural beauty is. Their eyes followed the flow of the fall down from the cliff to the pool below, where the red-haired woman was bathing. As James watched, she turned towards him, gazing into his eyes with her naked body on show. The sun glistened off her bosom, but there was another body in the water that attracted his attention. After a few moments, the long slender body peeked out of the water, and wrapped around the woman.

The large python-like snake caressed her body as it worked its way past her torso and over her breasts and shoulders; finally she raised her arms and lifted part of the serpent above her head. The serpent's head turned towards her face, not menacing, but more of a moment that lovers would share.

"You having a good look?" Tamara snapped at James.

"What?" He quickly shifted his attention to Tamara. "No…wait, did you see…?" He looked back at the pool, but this time the red-haired woman was by herself in the water with her back to the couple.

James was perplexed and confused and considered for a moment about disclosing to Tamara the vivid image he had just witnessed, but dismissed it as vulgar imagination of an overworked and exhausted mind.

4. Celebrations continue

At 9 pm, after much deliberation and debate, both James and Tamara left their room to attend the night's celebrations. Reaching the lobby of the Elder Inn, they saw the fifty-odd people from the previous night's parade in attendance, all dressed in white cotton robes. Sammy was the first to greet them, ushering them in with a drink in hand.

"Word to the wise, if you don't want to get drunk too quickly, don't have any of the red punch." Meanwhile, he took a sip of his glass filled to the brim with red punch.

The couple walked to the drinks table and assessed the two large bowls of punch, a yellow one and a red one. They followed Sammy's advice and poured two glasses of the yellow punch. James was first to have a taste of the drink.

"It's fruit, hardly any alcohol, it's all right," he reassuringly advised Tamara.

After she investigated the other guests' glasses filled with red punch, she felt more comfortable to take her first sip too.

After an hour or so had passed, and a few refreshing glasses of the fruit punch, James and Tamara had split up and were mingling with different people at the party. Tamara with Sammy and his wife, whilst James was with three men he didn't know, but all of whom were intoxicated beyond comprehension. James could all but nod and laugh on cue to fit in.

Just then the red-haired woman walked past his line of sight, between him and Tamara. To James she seemed to move in slow motion, with her straight hair flowing slightly and her white robe trailing behind, pressed up against her torso, revealing her slender body clearly. They exchanged a long intoxicated look, where she smiled, and for a moment James recalled that in the morning she did not look this young and attractive. Something about the way the lights were illuminating her skin and the flow of the white robe seemed to awaken something primal within. As she passed, Tamara disappeared from his view, as did Sammy and his wife. He didn't seem to mind, however, as if a comforting voice inside was confirming that she was okay.

As James took another sip of his drink, the whole room and everyone in it slowed to half speed. The volume dropped to where his own breathing and pulse were louder, and everyone's voice blurred into a general oscillating hum. He noticed that where people were once standing, they were now laid out on the floor with robes being removed, revealing naked bodies beneath. What ensued was a wicked and terrible display of human impulses being explored with complete recklessness.

A hand landed on James's shoulder and a whisper in his ear to follow him; he felt himself propelled and drawn out of the Elder Inn. He turned one last time before exiting and caught a glimpse of Tamara. She was nestled between Sammy and John, all three naked and engrossed in an act that James wished he had never laid eyes upon.

James found himself walking towards the church. The night breeze was cooling his face, a refreshing breeze after the steamy warmth of the lobby at the inn. He walked up the stairs and on the Gateway Stone, which tonight did not affect him the way it did earlier in the day. The doors were open and he stepped in. It was dark and it took a moment for him to adjust his vision. But soon the moonlight beamed through the windows to light up the church. In the centre, surrounded by the statues, stood the red-haired woman. He felt an urge in his right hand lifting the glass of yellow drink to his lips. He drank the remainder of glass, and fell deeper into the induced stupor.

He peered down at the empty glass and noticed his shadow on the floor, which he found strange as neither the statues nor the red-haired woman cast a shadow to be seen.

He didn't know if this was real or an illusion, but in the coma-induced state that he was in, the lines between the two were blurred and devoid. She peeled off her robe and it fell to the floor by her feet, revealing her white skin, willing him on to join her in the middle of the circle. He stumbled forward through no will of his own and walked towards her, knowing exactly what would happen, but he had no way of stopping himself.

He found himself, moments later, naked with his body pressed against hers, on the floor looking up, and she mounted him. The ecstasy he felt was unlike anything he had ever felt before. After a few moments, more pressing matters caused his eyes to wonder around the room. The statues now looked more alive than ever; they threatened to move from their base seemingly leaning forward to take their first step. The room started to spin and the statues started to sway and gawk as the red-haired woman continued to pleasure his body and her own.

His knowing mind wanted to scream at the horrors that it began to witness. The serpent statue swam off its base and floated in the air as if in the depths of the ocean, swimming and slithering overhead. It swam down towards them and started to wrap around the red-haired woman's body. For a moment the two figures merged into one, her face replaced by the grotesque one of the serpent god.

It was at this moment where any sane man would have reached his limits and the reality of what he knowingly witnessed became a sight too far, as such it did for James, and everything faded into darkness and silence. He could hear his heart beat and his lungs inhaling and exhaling deep breaths, but even those started to fade slowly as his mind and body extinguished, limp and motionless.

5. The morning after

The heat from the morning sun blazed through the window and the room illuminated revealing the loose dust in the air. James started to open his eyes, but the sunlight was blinding and he had to reach for the window to close the curtains to filter out the harsh brightness. He was slightly disorientated by the rude awakening, but he tried to clear his head. He turned to Tamara, who was under the covers but seemed to be awakening as she rustled under the sheets.

James felt his heart skip multiple beats as the horror unfolded when he removed the sheet, revealing the goat spirit god lying next to Tamara. It had its mouth open and wrapped around her temple, biting, crushing and swallowing Tamara's head. The bones were breaking and cracking, her face deforming with each movement of the goat's jaws. Tamara was passed out, either dead or under a trance, but she did not move or struggle against the goat, and James could only watch for a few more moments before he screamed and scrambled off the bed.

The heat from the morning sun blazed through the window and the room illuminated, revealing the loose dust in the air. James started to open his eyes, but the sunlight was blinding and he had to reach for the window to close the curtains to filter out the harsh brightness. He had sweat beads on his forehead after the fantastically terrible nightmare.

He knew for sure the image of Tamara and the goat was indeed a dream. But what about the night before, his lust filled adventure with the red-haired woman and the serpent god coming to life? Was that dream, or reality?

Something was not right; for a start Tamara was missing, and his room looked bare besides the clothes that had been draped over the chair. He couldn't see his bags, or any of their belongings, and the town seemed very quiet this morning. He peered outside the window, the streets were empty, with no activity, and all of the shops were closed. Checking his watch, he was even more perplexed as it read three in the afternoon. With a head full of questions and an unexplained lack of concern about his missing wife Tamara, he prepared himself and left his room.

Arriving downstairs he noticed Harold was not at the front desk, nor was there a trace of anyone being in the hotel. His car, however, was parked outside and the tyres were fine. He sat in the driver's seat and turned the engine over—it started fine. He decided to drive back to the bridge, so he put the car in gear and proceeded to perform a three-point turn. As he drove very slowly he noticed that the shops were empty and didn't have signs. They were deserted and some were even boarded up, but the church remained as he remembered it in the rear-view mirror. He drove past the shops and the few residential houses, but couldn't see the bridge yet as the road descended down beyond view.

He slowed his pace even more when the road beyond came into view and a shocking sight followed. He had reached lands' end, a few metres ahead was a cliff and a violent ocean below. He stepped out of the car, and an overwhelming feeling of helplessness took over—he neither understood nor had any solutions for what he was witnessing. He followed the coastline on his left and noticed that it continued around, dipping down to reveal a deserted beach below. The coastline on his right ascended up to a higher mountain range not more than a few hundred metres away. There was no sign of any civilisation in either direction.

Driving back through the street towards the church, he sped up—he had focus now. He drove past the church, and arrived at a dirt path, with dense trees on both sides, which he remembered from the previous day when they headed towards the fountain and pool. He left the car behind as he walked down the path to what he expected to be the fountain. After a few minutes of hiking he noticed a clearing, and as he got closer he was met with a similar shocking sight, another cliff edge.

Further unsettling was that to the left he saw a shallow drop to a beach below. He then followed the rocks rise up to the mountain range: the very same mountains he saw from the previous vantage point. He turned his head to the right, and much the same as the left, the coastline seemed to meet up with the end points he could see from the previous lookout.

He had to take a moment to question his first thoughts, as the conclusion seemed ridiculous. However, the more he tried to dismiss it, the more he realised his efforts were futile. He was in fact on an island.

The more this reality dawned and sank in, the more

James felt he was losing his mind. The lines between reality and dreams were disappearing, as was his mental stability. In an effort to compose his senses, he closed his eyes and took a few deep breaths to calm his nerves and centre his thoughts. Upon opening his eyes he was not met with a different sight, but a slightly altered resolve.

He headed back into town; apart from the missing people, the decay and boarded up shops, nothing was amiss, including the church. In fact, he now gave more attention to the fact that the church was the only aspect of the town that had not changed from yesterday. Just then he noticed that the bar in the hotel still had drinks on the shelves. This was something of a welcomed surprise.

He retrieved the bottle of Bushmills Black, brushed away the dirt and popped the cork; it smelled fine and he had a taste, followed by a big gulp. The familiarity of the taste and the bottle was the only real experience he had that day and it gave him the perspective and confidence he needed to go on. With the newfound vitality, he decided to investigate the church.

He arrived at the steps of the church, not a detail out of place, yet the consistency was less comforting than he would have thought. He climbed the steps and, like the previous night, the Gateway Stone had no impact on him. He pushed the doors, at first struggling to move them, until one of the hinges gave way and both doors swung open and came to a sudden crash against the inner walls of the church. Inside, the sights were the same, the same gods in the circle, the same disturbing patterns on the windows and walls, but the cleanliness and freshness of the statues was missing.

Today the contents of the church looked old, with cracks and chips from the years of decay and lack of maintenance in general. There was nothing more to learn from the church beside the fact that the church had suffered the same fate as the rest of the town.

As he turned to leave he heard a footstep. He swivelled around on the balls of his feet as quickly as he could, ready for anything. Standing at the far end of the circle was the red-haired woman, dressed in the white cotton robe. James was astounded by her presence, but his mind was slightly more prepared for strange occurrences today than any other time in his life.

The-red haired woman approached James. "Why are you here, James? Why did you come to Larwock?" she said as she circled around him.

"We took a wrong turn…" he said.

"We, James? You are here by yourself," the red-haired woman interrupted.

James felt less sure of himself, but was quick to get his thoughts on the right track.

"By myself…no…no, I came here with Tamara, we got married and we were going down to Melbourne for a week…and we took a wrong…"

Just then James stopped and started to digest what he was saying. Thoughts started circling his brain, thoughts that were not once there, he questioned himself. "Who is Tamara?" and "When did I get married?"

The red-haired woman now stood face to face with James. "Why did you come back?" she whispered.

James was completely perplexed by the line of questioning.

"What do you mean? Who do you think I am?"

"James Green!" she whispered again.

James recalled the reference to the surname; he'd heard about Mr Green from Sammy at the café. He was the misfit leader of the coven of witches that escaped and found solace in this town. He was the man that protected the town by conjuring up all types of demons and spirits to roam the woods. The man who imagined these creatures, which were then turned into statues for the church. Now, she was saying that he was James Green, but how could this be? How could there be any truth to this?

In his bewildered state James stumbled back out of the church. He stepped onto the Gateway Stone and a sudden onset of vertigo thrust him off balance and he leapt off the deck and landed head-first on the road, blacking out on impact.

6.   The final feast

"Wake up, James…James…are you okay? James!"

His vision was blurred, but he caught glimpses of her angelic face and felt the warm caress of her hands on his face. Like a mother's familiar touch, he felt the safety and comfort that only a loved one could provide.

Tamara stroked his face again, and noticing his eyes flickering open, she smiled. "James…you're back…are you okay?" she said with a tender tone.

James finally opened his eyes and his vision was restored, but the pain he felt shooting up from his parietal all the way to his sinus took its place. He lifted his head with discomfort and was aided to a seated position. Reaching to the back of his head, he felt the warm blood that had started to trickle down through his hair.

James gazed up at Tamara, a vision of beauty and relief, but then his eyes wandered to her right—the red-haired woman, Harold and Sammy. He immediately jumped to his feet.

"Tamara, we have to go…NOW!" James took Tamara by complete surprise with his urgent tone.

"But James, our car has punctured tyres and John won't have tyres till tomorrow… What's wrong, James? You look like you've seen a ghost."

"I've seen much, much worse!" he said.

Tamara was concerned, firstly about his uncharacteristic reaction, but also there was something more to his demand, something urgent. She was inclined to go along with him and ask for explanations later. She nodded and began to follow him as he turned away.

"You can't go anywhere now. Please, James, you're hurt. Why don't you rest the night and leave tomorrow…" the red-haired women tried to reason with him.

James turned to her with disgust; every word from her mouth was like poison to him and he didn't restrain his emotions this time.

"You…you're a deceitful snake." He spewed the insult from his mouth like the vilest vomit.

"James, calm down, mate. I don't know what happened, but when you and Tamara were trying to get into the church you slipped and fell on your head…you've been knocked out for about ten minutes now. I think it's best you take a seat, maybe lie down…don't you think?" Sammy was trying to calm the situation, which had obviously gotten out of control.

James had no time for excuses, however. "I've seen every-thing…I know what this place is…and we are getting out of here…"

Before James could continue, both Tamara and James were startled by the ginger-haired man, Steve, who stepped out of the hotel and was upon the couple.

"Hello Mr Green." Steve's words rang in James's ear like church bells.

"What?" James turned to Steve. "No, I'm not Mr Green. My name is James Diamine…"

Steve scratched his temple, and then he pointed to the red-haired woman. "Well, the good lady there said that you were."

James peered over his shoulder at the red-haired woman again. "I knew I wasn't dreaming…you WITCH!" But his victorious revelation was soon extinguished.

"James, your mum's maiden name was Green, right?" Tamara said as if she had known this was coming all along.

James's head began spinning and the truth behind all of this was now starting to come to light. He was part of the bloodline. Although he didn't want to admit it to himself, his dreams were not merely dreams, they were all visions of the truth. The red-haired woman was a witch who somehow had controlled his mind with all those images. He returned his focus to his new bride, his one love, Tamara, but her face was distorting. His brain was racing with thoughts, and it all became too much to process.

Tamara smiled at her husband, but soon it turned into laughter. Was this real, or was he back in his dreams? Why was Tamara laughing along with the others? The sound of the laughter became louder and louder until it became the only thing he could hear. His vision blurred as Tamara released his hand and he seemed to spiral in the middle of the road. He was surrounded by the townsfolk, who looked like a pack of hungry wolves staring at their wounded prey.

"I am Mr Green…I am Mr Green…I am Mr Green…" James kept repeating it over and over again.

His legs lost the strength to hold his weight. But before he fell to the ground, Steve lifted him over his shoulder and took him into the hotel, where the other town folk and Tamara followed.

Inside the lobby of the Elder Inn, Tamara lifted the carpet to reveal a large pentagram engraved into the floor boards. Steve placed James in the middle of the circle. James was delirious, his mind warped and twisted by the events to its limits. His conscious mind slipped back and lost control over his body, his thoughts and reactions. He laid limp on the floor staring at the ceiling.

In this wild state it wasn't long before the carved outlines of the gods on the ceiling took shape and reanimated. Twisting in the air around him, they seemed pleased with his arrival and approving of what was about to take place.

James shifted his view to Steve, who was now walking towards him with a long sharp knife. He could feel a voice inside him willing him, pleading with him, to stand up and run, to raise his feet and kick Steve, but none of these cries were acted upon. James witnessed his shirt being torn apart and with the precision of a surgeon, Steve cut a line from the top of his chest all the way down to his pelvis.

James was beyond pain, or anything else a normal human would feel, his mind in a place that only dead men wander and only madness survives. He could hear mutterings, but the voice of the red-haired woman was the most noticeable at this time as she spoke ahead of everyone.

"Ahriman, we praise you, and offer this soul back to you again. We thank you for blessing us with your servant Tamara, for it was she who brought back the descendant of our leader, the great communicator, so we can feast on his flesh and send his soul back to Ahriman's elder gods…"

In the meantime, Steve had made another incision from one kidney to the other, and had fallen back into the circle.

The red-haired woman kneeled to the floor over James's dissected body. She gently ran her hand into his body and cupped it, collecting a small amount of blood. With lustful eyes and insatiable thirst she drank the blood and raised her bloodied hands in the air.

"Ahriman, take this soul back and through his flesh, grant us our immortality and your protection!"

James began to fade, but his consciousness was returning and the madness was subsiding in the last moments of life. The crowd chanted in a foreign tongue as they slowly crept towards him, their eyes growing with hunger and rabid aggression. Among them he spotted Tamara; she was no different from the others. The horde of animals were moments away and he didn't fight the darkness that was now starting to approach. He closed his eyes, but the darkness was not so quick to arrive.

The pain from the gashes made their way through all the receptors in his brain, the recognition was coming too early, and he wished this would all end.

But before it did, he opened his eyes one last time, only to get one last glimpse of the pack of ravenous cannibals descending into his open torso.

Calling for help

She recalled five years ago, almost to the day, she started her journey of discovery. The discovery of her father's only aim in life, the mythical history he was chasing to bring to reality. She wondered whether today would be bearing the fruit of all the research over the past five years. As she sat by the phone, building the courage to make the phone call, she reminisced about the first time she learnt about the horrors and queer life that lay beyond her own simple reality.

Shannon arrived at the house of her late father in the morning. She had been called a week earlier to come back to her childhood house in the south coast town of Jervis Bay. She didn't arrive in time for the funeral, not for a man that she had despised from an early age. But her family home was to be sold, and to avoid the cost of clearing the house, she decided to come back and clear it out herself.

The first time her father had left the family was when she was only eight. He would do this twice every year at least, going for periods of a month or longer. Her mother, while she was alive, would make up stories to alleviate Shannon's immediate emotional response. But once her mother passed away, there were no more stories. Shannon would be left to her own devices as a teenager, whilst her father would disappear randomly.

Even when her father was at home, their relationship was non-existent. He would tend to his own duties, leaving her to look after the house and herself. To her credit she managed to put herself through school and secure a place at the University of New South Wales. This was perfect as it was her way of escaping the house, the town and her father. She would have a new start in Sydney and rebuild her life, independent of the dysfunctional family unit that she was a part of.

But now she was back in the house and those memories were starting to flood back. Every item in that house was almost as she had left it and reminded her of an event or an emotion. Besides the few that brought her mother back to life, the rest were memories that she had tried to forget over the last ten years or so.

She started in her bedroom, a room she spent most of her life in. Not in the same way as most children; in this case, Shannon hardly ever left her bedroom. In here, she found a sanctuary, where she could pretend to have a normal life and a father who loved her. Outside those walls was a world that was not perfect or remotely close to it.

There was, however, one room in the house that she had never ventured into: the library, a small room where her father spent most of his time and years in. Outside being vacant from the family, the rest of the time he would spend in this room, staying up till late at night. Shannon never asked or wanted to know what he did in that room and was happy not being involved. Today, however, the curiosity was growing in her mind, and although she kept to her room most of the day, she knew at some stage she would have to enter that room.

She stayed overnight at the old house, and her boyfriend, Edward, joined her for the night. They planned to stay there for the weekend, to salvage as much as possible before the cleaners would come and clear out the house and get it ready for sale.

The next day, she knew, would be the day she would

venture into that unknown room at the back of the house. It faced on to the back garden, but the windows were painted black, with two or three coats of thick tar-like paint. No light could get in and no prying eyes could see what was happening in that room. From the inside a door with a lock kept her and her mother out of that room for as long as they lived in the house.

Edward had to use some brute force to smash the door open, but it took little effort given the age of the wood and house. Inside was a sight that she had not expected. A mess of papers, maps and books lay open and in random order on the table and floor. On first impression there was no order to the madness, but after a few minutes, she found some kind of pattern.

Each map lay next to some notes that were scattered around it. These maps seemed to be of one particular area, a town called Bowral, west of Wollongong. But also, each map seemed to be of a different time in history; some were ripped out of historical books, some were hand drawn, and some were more recent print-outs from computer generated images.

She picked up a random set of notes, and began reading.

"Today I will set off for the third time. This map shows a position in the bushland off the western border of Bowral. I'm not sure if this is the right way; right now I am trying to eliminate directions rather than find the right one. The Aboriginal tribes that lived nearby originally travelled on this particular path. When I spoke to Geoff, he told me that his father had told him stories when he was younger about the death trail. A trail that the evil ones would walk to their death, once they were outcast from their tribe.

"They believed in this so much, that this area of bushland became no-man's land, and if anyone did by accident venture into the bushland during a hunt they would die a few days later. Back in those days they believed that evil spirits touched them. Geoff told me that the tribes were so convinced of the evil, that they would will themselves to death."

Shannon was completely perplexed at what she had read, more so, however, when she read the date at the top of the page, a date she recalls her father leaving. She remembered this one because her school netball team was due to play in the state championship for under thirteens. This was the most exciting event of her life, at the time, and to this day she remembered the feeling of winning the game, only to find that her father was not there to congratulate her.

She moved onto another set of notes, inspecting the date first, and correlating it again with another time that he had left the family for a prolonged period of time. Similar mysterious notes about finding an area on a map and trying to discover something followed.

This was proving to be a momentous discovery for Shannon. After many years she was suddenly getting an insight into her father and what he spent, as it seemed, most of his life chasing. From first impressions, Shannon had concluded he was obviously mad.

"What is all this, Shaz?" Edward broke the long silence.

"Don't worry, Eddy…you go do the living room and I'll finish in here. If you see a badly made ashtray, with the word 'Mum' on it, put it in the box to take home with us," Shannon replied as she circled around to the table.

"Sure." Edward left the room and headed down the hall.

Shannon sat behind the table, with five sets of papers laid

out. In the middle she found an old journal, which did not seem to be her father's. This journal was too old, and the handwriting too nice to be his. The paper had a dark patina and the ink in parts had faded. It had been written with ink, most likely fountain pen, but a dipping fountain pen, as every now and again the line seemed to start with heavy flowing ink and it tapered away as the ink had run out.

The journal seemed to be that of a barber, as it chronicled the day's work and idle gossip that the barber would hear on the day. But going back to the page that was open when she found it, a few pages from the end, she noticed that the writing had become erratic and somewhat clumsy. However, this seemed to be the most interesting part of the book and the part that gave some clues as to her father's work.

On the last entry, the journal read like a cry for help of some kind. But the message was queer and fictional. She continued reading regardless.

"I'm stuck here now. I have days where I am alive and others when I'm not. I try to reach out, but I'm not here. I don't know where I am.

"I need help.

"I am calling out to my kin, my child, the child of my child and even beyond. I don't know how long I've been here. I don't know if I am dead or alive.

"Today I am myself, but I don't know when the last time was when I was myself. I lose track of time here, I don't even know what year this is anymore.

"I am under a spell that I can't break. All I remember is walking west, but it was past the witching hour and the caravan took us on enough turns to lose our bearings. Too many events took place for me to remember exactly where we went.

"I hope this place exists, and whoever finds this book can find me and set me free."

Shannon put the book down, and sat back to think of what this meant and why it became the work of her father to find this man.

From there she progressed to her father's other books and notebooks specifically. Reading what he had learnt from the books and the experiments he carried out to prove the truth; a truth that only he knew of, a dangerous reality that threatened existence and morality.

She learnt that her father and his father before him had taken this path of discovery and this was something of a family heritage. But both had failed; yet they had small victories. Her grandfather found the old notebook, and her father had discovered a book of sorcery that was connected to this myth.

It soon dawned on her that she was next; her father had left all of his research within easy access and order for her to find it. He meant for her to continue it. He had sacrificed fatherhood for a greater mission, and Shannon, although she struggled with the idea, began to understand it. She was next and she would have to carry out what they could not.

Five years ago, this awakening was the single most important event in her life. She drew meaning in life, with a purpose far beyond the daily drudgery of the commercial world and insignificance of material belongings and careers. She focused her attention on one purpose. She was the one that would destroy Larwock and those fiends that occupied it.

Birth of a town

1. The strange case of Mr Green

It must have been over a hundred years ago now, when a commune packed their caravans, fed their horses and went on their long journey across the dark forest to set up their new home. The reasons behind the journey weren't so innocent, however; they were escaping a harrowing fate. But the persecution wasn't uncalled for; in fact it was a necessity and an act of self-defence. This commune of misfits was a cult led by a man who partook in the darkest of magic whilst under influence of drugs of every nature.

Mr Green was the name he was known by, a man of mysterious power with an unknown past to most people, but feared and revered all at the same time. His past, however, was less spectacular than most believe, apart from one particular incident that made him the man he became.

He was born to farmers; as an only child, he was pampered more than he should have been. At the age of twelve he developed a strange illness, which robbed him the use of his legs, and he was reduced to sitting, or struggling on homemade crutches. The kind of medical assistance he required was not afforded to him.

In his solitary despair, Mr Green took an unhealthy

dislike towards the human race and the world as it was.

His hatred led him to researching the dark arts, and given the amount of free time he had, his knowledge grew fast and deep. This growing solitude was of concern to his ageing and overtired parents. Most other farmers in the area would pass the hard work to their children once they were of age and thus wouldn't slave on the land in their elder years. However, the Greens didn't have that luxury, and the daily grind along with the grief and worry finally took their toll on the couple. Firstly his father died at the age of 42, and only four years later his mother passed at the age of 41.

Mr Green was left to his own devices by the age of 19, head full of the darkest knowledge and a body still confined to a chair. What happened next for the young man was the defining moment, however; a peculiar event that determined not only his fate but all those who joined him and his commune.

On a night where the locals were sure they had heard farm animals on the Green farm screaming and desperately trying to escape, there was a thunderstorm. One eye witness who passed the story on was a young boy in a neighbouring farm, who sat at his bedroom window watching the storm. He was amazed by the sight as he had been from a young age. Unlike other young children who would run to their mother's side, this young boy found the experience enthralling. It's because of his gaze that we know what happened next to Mr Green.

The sequence of events that the boy explained to his father was dismissed at first, but on subsequent days when his father witnessed the results for himself, he became a believer and began to spread the story through the town. The story was embellished and whispers altered, but the general theme was all the same. Subsequently the fantastical nature of the events was conserved within everyone's retelling of that strange night.

The boy was taking great care in watching and listening to the thunderstorm. He would listen for the sound of thunder and begin to count sets of three second intervals to determine the distance of the lightning from his location. Even though the sound made him jump, he enjoyed the sensation, and kept a keen eye on the clouds. But one thing made his focus falter, when he saw Mr Green struggling out of his house to the paddock on his poorly made crutches. The mud and wind made this a very difficult trip, but through sheer grit and determination he managed to pull himself a good ten feet away from his house.

Once there, the boy swears that the thunder subsided and clouds began to move quicker and not in one linear direction, but in one direction towards each other, clustering above the Green farm. Then he heard Mr Green scream out some form of chant, repeating it over and over, with his voice becoming louder with each repetition. Moving his focus to the clouds, the boy noticed the wind swirling and picking up light debris, spinning it around Mr Green. Meanwhile he started hearing the slow and low rumbling of thunder as if it was building up to something hazardous.

After a few moments, the storm seemed to be at full strength and in an instant a lightning rod shot down from the centre of the clouds along with a deafening sound that made the boy jump back and his ears hum. His eyes, however, were unaffected and he witnessed the event. The lightning had found Mr Green and was upon him like a beacon, illuminating his whole body as he shook under the great power of the lightning.

The boy said it went on for minutes, but most likely only a few seconds; even still, any man would have surely perished from this intense charge. The boy then told his father that, when the lightning dissipated to the ground, Mr Green was still standing, and very much alive. He did go down to his knees for a short moment, but then he stood up, victorious.

The boy remembered that Mr Green then raised his hands in the air, thanking the storm, as the clouds and thunder subsided and was replaced with clear night skies. Mr Green then picked up his crutches and threw them as far as he could muster. Rejuvenated, he strode with pride into his house, and all was quiet in the sky and on the Green farm.

2. The seeds of evil

Much had happened in the twelve years since Mr Green miraculously restored his legs, and for the most part what had happened was seen to be evil and blasphemous. It began with the weekly gatherings on the Green farm. At first it started with one or two people, but before long it grew to approximately fifty, over the years.

Then there was the farm itself. Mr Green did not grow any crops and his animals had either died through starvation or escaped, but he did somehow foster the growth of a special breed of mushrooms throughout his property. These mushrooms were harvested at the start of each weekly meeting, consumed at the events, and by the following week had regrown completely.

The locals put this down to devil worship and witchcraft, but harmless to those outside the circle. They knew that the meetings were purely drug-fuelled orgies and that was the extent of it all—and to their credit they were mostly correct. What they didn't know was what these orgies were in aid of and what the result would be.

The local church's weekly sermons always included some reference to the Green farm and what took place, urging the congregation to stay clear of the farm and the people involved. Even the Reverend steered clear of the farm or contact with the people involved.

The town became divided into two parts, with even the local businesses biased towards either side. Mr Green's people shopped at their own stores and drank in their own pub, whilst the other shops and the other pub in town were the domain of the rest of the town folk. There was an uneasy tension between the two groups, which in the most part was peaceful, with currents of mistrust and some fear running beneath the surface. But it all changed when a special young woman came into town, from parts unknown.

There were fantastic rumors that she was not of this earth; that she had come from the sea and was summoned by Mr Green. Strangers did not frequent this part of the world very often, especially ones who wandered into the town unannounced, wearing only a white cotton robe and carrying no baggage. She was alone, without a name and without a place to live, but somehow she walked through the town quietly and with purpose, making no mistake in direction as she arrived at the front door of the Green farmhouse. Some folk even followed her to see what would happen next, but their fear didn't allow them to get too close to know exactly what happened, except to say that she was welcomed into the house like a long-lost relative.

The men were more taken by the arrival than their wives, mostly drawn to her natural beauty and the glow of her perfect white skin. The day she arrived was like a dream; she glided through the street, her white robe floating in the trailing wind. Her straight red hair blew gently in the breeze, dancing in the air like fairies. Her posture was perfect and she looked ahead, never breaking stride as her bare feet walked over the dirt road that ran through the middle of town. Even though her glide was silent, the men were drawn to the store windows as if witnessing a storm rushing through the centre of town. They gawked, memorised by her beauty, but she did not notice any of the attention afforded to her by the men, and she carried on.

The Green farm was never the same after the red-haired woman arrived; it was already strange, but now it was beyond the boundaries of tolerance. The fungi that created the mushrooms on a weekly basis released a stench now, which travelled throughout the town and into other houses. Every Thursday morning as if on cue, the town would be overtaken by the stench of the mushrooms, and it continued till Friday night when they were harvested. The meetings now became louder and harrowing screams could be heard from the house. It wasn't long before the followers never left the Green farm and the nightly rituals ensued relentlessly.

The town folk knew they would have to take action. But their underlying fear relegated the actions to thoughts and quiet discussions rather than any real response to the danger. This was all until the night of May 31, 1905, the night their fears created enough courage, born out of self-preservation and survival, that they banded together against the misfits that had plagued their town for too long.

3. Disaster at Mount Kembla

Months before the end of May in 1905, the red-haired woman arrived, unannounced and unknown to all in the town. No one ventured to seek her out or learn her name or past, just rumours and strange tales of the imagination followed her into the town and in the minds of the town folk. But one thing known for sure was that she knew she was there for a reason and in the whole time leading to the event in May she was never seen leaving the Green farm. Which made it even stranger in the people's minds, as some speculated that she was sent by a dark lord and was sacrificed during one the weekly debaucheries that went on at the Green farm.

Among the many stories that circled the town, each one trying to outdo the other, there was a familiar thread that could be laced together. No one was sure where any of the stories originated from; some say they saw certain things and some were just misunderstood whispers, but there were some common threads. The wiser of the town folk, those less likely to succumb to idle gossip and slandering, actually took some time to hear the stories and try to research the basis for each one and come to a conclusion as to the truths and exaggerations. One man who did such a task, Steve Cooling, ran the local barber shop and was privy to hearing every rumour and story in town.

After hearing all the stories he decided he would go to some of the places mentioned in the stories and see if these stories had any basis in truth, and in some cases he was surprised that the weirdest tales actually carried more weight than others. Slowly, he created a log of each tale and put together his thoughts on each one. By the end, he had a story of the red-haired woman, and he told this story to a few, who told it on and before long this became the tale of Charlene Everette.

Charlene was not a strange creature or a product of any conjuration, but a bastard child of a mining family from Mount Kembla, a town just outside Wollongong. Her father was one of the miners, and her mother was the daughter of the local inn keeper. This particular inn keeper was a ruthless and cold man who disowned his daughter once she was pregnant and threw her to the streets. With nowhere to turn, the daughter left, and found solace in an abandoned cabin on the outskirts of town.

She was never visited by family, as her father had forbidden it, and she never entered town for fear of retribution. Although it was no secret she was living in the cabin, it was a mystery, however, how she managed to give birth and raise her child by herself, with no medical aid or otherwise.

Her daughter Charlene grew to the age of fifteen in that cabin without once entering the town. They lived off what the forest provided and from time to time they would hunt small rodents and possums to supplement an otherwise vegetarian diet. However, in 1902, at the age of fifteen, Charlene was forced to leave their solace of peace and isolation and enter the town. Her mother had been sick for some time and she had no choice but to seek the aid of modern medicine. On July 29th she left their cabin and ventured into town hoping to come back and mend her mother, the only person she had known in this world.

On foot, she travelled through the forest for over a day and arrived tired and hungry on July 30th. Charlene was completely overwhelmed by the city of Mount Kembla. She had lived with one person her whole life, and in a city with hundreds of people rushing from one place to another was a sight she had never witnessed before. Her mother, however, had taught her to read, so she scanned the stores and street signs as she walked through the town, but didn't notice the populous scanning her. She was unaware of the thoughts that were going through their minds as they looked upon her unblemished young white skin, loosely covered by a white robe, contrasting against her long red hair. To say she was out of place with the coal-stained workers and hard skinned women of this town would be a grave understatement.

She endured until she stumbled upon the local pharmacy. Inside she met and was comforted by the pharmacist, who was also one of the town doctors. He assured her that it was not a serious illness, given the symptoms, and that he would mix the medicine the next day and he would accompany her to their cabin to consult her mother. Her polite nature and genuine gratitude for his assistance was enough reason for him to agree to make this trip without charge, and so she decided to stay the night at the inn.

Charlene checked into the inn in the afternoon, and had her dinner whilst the miners were drowning another day of sweat-filled work with cold beers. The more they drank the more their interest in the young red-haired woman grew, and the more their voices travelled to her ears. She rushed her dinner and made her way up the stairs to her room, catching an evil glance from one of the miners on the way.

Once in her room she barricaded the door with a dressing table and a chair, and she sat on her bed listening to the voices of the miners below echoing up the stairwell and into her room. Their drunken lust was turning them into animals as they bellowed scenarios where they would have their way with the young girl. But this was not all talk, for after what seemed like twenty minutes there was a knock on her door, followed by a gentle turn of the door knob. She did not dare answer the door, she knew who was there and she could hear the shuffling feet of drunken men outside her room.

Finally there was one, then two big shoulder thrusts to the door, the first one blasting the door ajar, and the second one pushing the furniture to the side and opening the door wide and free of obstructions. Charlene screamed, but there was no help in sight, as five miners stood at her door, grinning with all the dastardly intentions in their minds. What happened next needs no explanation, only to mention that this was a mistake that those miners and the town would never forget.

The miners' pleasure was shortlived, as even a ruthless unloving grandfather can only stand so much. The inn keeper, with rifle in hand, rushed the miners out of the room, firing the gun once to make sure they would leave and never come back. He then looked upon his granddaughter, silent and in shock with torn clothes. Blood was dotted on her white robe and tears were running down her face. The mirror image of the daughter that he threw out into the street fifteen years earlier, and now his granddaughter raped and abused in his inn. The inn keeper broke down to his knees, shame and grief taking over his whole being. Years of guilt and sadness all to save his pride and reputation, and this was the result.

Charlene was beyond any kind of family reunion; the hate and anger she now possessed pushed her to her feet. She approached the inn keeper and put her hand over his head, and at that instant he felt a noose around his heart shooting pain throughout his body. She raised her other hand above her head, chanting in some ancient tongue, calling down for strength and bidding for something to be done in her name. Following this, people at the inn recalled a small tremor, not an earthquake, but just a very small shaking that lasted for approximately half a minute and then subsided. They then recalled the young girl walking down the stairs and out of the inn, and disappearing into the dark night at the edges of the town, never to be seen again.

The next day in Mount Kembla there was a disaster that shadows the town to this day: the mining disaster of 1902. There was speculation about what occurred and what caused the explosion in the mine that took the lives of so many miners and left widows and fatherless children in the town. The primary reason reported was the release of gas in the mines sometime the night before. A speculative theory at the time, as the mine was known for being gas-free and safe, but later the evidence was conclusive to the presence of gas. But no one could ascertain where the gas had come from, and how the gas penetrated the mines of Mount Kembla.

4. Grimoire of Ahriman

The next part of the story, Steve Cooling actually heard from the doctor himself, when he made the trip to Mount Kembla. The doctor remembered the events and recalled it with some fear and a tremble in his voice. He remembered on the day of the explosion, he was first called to the inn as the inn keeper had died from a heart attack. Upon finishing his work there, he still made the trip to see Charlene's mother, but he was met with more sorrow as Charlene's mother had passed during the night.

At first the doctor thought the symptoms of the infection were accelerated, but upon further inspection he concluded she too had been struck with a heart attack. But that wasn't the most troubling thing in the abandoned cabin, as he also saw a book by her bedside table.

In fact, besides the makeshift beds, the small table, and the book, there was nothing else in the cabin, which was strange given the two had lived there for so long. But, forgetting the somewhat large anomaly, he turned his attention to the book. The black leatherbound book was tattered and rough, yet still sturdy. He opened the book to reveal the title, in a strange text that was a series of short vertical and horizontal lines. He had no idea what it was, but knew of someone in town who might: a professor of geology and archaeology, who worked for the mining company.

That night, amongst the madness in the town, the doctor sat at his dining room table with Professor Dickson, who inspected the book through his reading glasses. He opened the book and inspected the title, at which point he took his glasses off and looked up at the doctor accusingly.

"Where did you get this book, Gerald?" he said in a short and unforgiving tone.

The doctor reiterated the story honestly and assured him of the truthfulness of it, which seemed to appease the professor. He looked down at the book again and randomly flicked through some pages. He looked up again.

"This book is very dangerous. I assume you have no idea what this book is about and where it's from?"

The doctor shrugged, so the professor continued.

"Gerald, you've stumbled onto something quite evil here, and between you and me, I am glad the owner of this book is dead and her daughter has left town. Loosely translated, it's *The Grimoire of Ahriman*. It's an ancient Persian book of sorcery."

The doctor smiled at the ridiculous nature of the book. "Surely, professor, you don't believe this stuff is real. I mean, I don't doubt that's what the book is about, but to think that there was any danger. I mean, it's 1902, not 1602…" The doctor smirked mockingly.

"Yes, I'm not saying magic is real." The professor laughed quietly, and then continued more seriously. "But anyone in possession of a book like this is a dangerous human being. The kind of madness that would believe in this kind evil is inherently evil. But, Gerald, although we are both men of science, there are still aspects of this earth that we can't explain. I'm not saying there is truth to this book, but deep down I can't discount it wholly. And for someone to have had this book for so long and to have passed it down generation after generation after generation…"

The doctor interrupted him at this stage, his interest piqued. "What do you mean generation to generation…? How old is this book?"

"Oh, I don't think this book is all that old. It's been hand copied from a previous version. I have no idea when the original owner had this book. But I can tell you this: a similar book, *Picatrix*, which was an Arabic book of sorcery, was written in the tenth century. Now, considering this is Persian and is written in text which is pre-Arabic invasion, when the Persians were Zoroastrians, it could be dated to any time before the year 650." The professor mused over the cover, trying to confirm the authenticity of what he had claimed.

Meanwhile, Gerald took a deep breath and sat back in his chair. But he was still puzzled and had one last question he thought. "So the Gremoire of Amri…"

The professor interrupted him quickly. "No, Gerald, it's *The Grimoire of Ahriman*, the name the Zoroastrians gave to their evil god, what the Arabs and Hebrews later called Shatan, and we call Satan…now, do you get why I was concerned?"

The reality of the situation suddenly sank in for the doctor and he realised how close he was to the kind of madness that only appears in dreams. But then his thoughts turned to the book itself and the small issue of him now having possession of it, which had such evil surrounding it.

He turned to the professor pleadingly. "Professor, with everything you've told me, to be honest, I don't really want this book in my house. Would you mind taking it?"

To his surprise, however, the professor had no reservations and was actually pleased at the notion, quickly nodding his head like a child accepting candy.

Once the doctor had told his story to Steve, he asked about the interest in Charlene and the events of that night, and was dually horrified when Steve informed him that she had arrived in their town. He pleaded with him that the town folk needed to take action and not let her stay there— she and her kind were not people that should walk amongst the living. Steve was not rattled; he wanted some reason for any kind of hasty action, like exiling a person from a town, and he was surely given one. The doctor then recounted to Steve the subsequent night at Mount Kembla.

The professor left the doctor's house that night with the book, and headed home for some late night reading and research into this historical artifact as he saw it. The doctor, meanwhile, had a glass of brandy before retiring to bed, trying to forget the horrors of the day and the sorrow that had befallen the town.

As he sat on his bed on the second floor above the pharmacy, he peered out the window. The town was quiet and the gas lamps in the street were emitting a yellow glow that was making its way through the dust still floating in the air from the explosion earlier in the day. From his room he could see to the next block, and the roof of the professor's house. He could see the light from his study where the professor was surely working.

But, as he was ready to turn in, he witnessed something that to this day caused shivers through his spine. He saw a shadow in the street, a shadow like a swirling snake travelling down the street, and the lamps flickering as the shadow passed. Behind the shadow, maybe ten paces back, he saw Charlene, robed in white, walking purposefully behind the abomination. He quickly turned out the candle and stood to his feet, watching this event unfold, completely captivated by it.

His knees soon grew weak and tears of fear ran down his face as Charlene turned her gaze upon him. She saw him, she knew he was there, and they locked eyes for an eternity it seemed. The doctor fell to his knees and his life flashed before his eyes; he felt her eyes threatening his very soul. After a moment and a warning he will never forget, she turned her head back to the shadow.

Then the doctor noticed another strange sight that haunted his dreams. As Charlene walked through the street, each street lamp she passed would flicker and then it would turn off. She extinguished all light behind her, leaving a deep evil darkness that even the moonlight couldn't illuminate.

He watched the shadow rise up into the air and travel over the houses and shops, whilst Charlene turned the corner and disappeared. The doctor followed the shadow as it ventured closer and closer to the professor's house and, finally, entering the chimney. The doctor was frozen with fear; the shadow had disappeared, and the doctor couldn't see into the professor's house. There was only one sign that he witnessed, a flickering of the light in the professor's study and then moments later, it extinguished, along with the professor's life.

The doctor was so distraught that he did not dare leave his house that night, but the next day he quickly made his way to the professor's house and found him dead in his study. There was no sign of struggle or anybody else being there. For coronary purposes the professor had died of a heart attack at his desk and fallen to the floor. At his desk were some papers, and one fresh paper with some notes that ended abruptly. The doctor remembered the note word for word, as the final harrowing words the professor had written just before his passing.

"This book has been in my possession for a few hours now, which has been little time for me to examine it thoroughly. My first impression is a strange one, which I hope does not make me sound a fool. But I must write this down as it's an emotion and a moment in time that should be captured.

"Since opening this book in my study, I have had a feeling that my body is being used as a form of communication. There is a distinct sensation in my mind that something is talking through me, out of this house, out of this town and maybe out of the planet and time. I am not sure who is listening and who will respond, but I feel something out there has heard this call and they are using me as a beacon.

"Perhaps reading this book may have been a mistake, and reading these first few phrases or at least translating them may have opened some door.

"I will continue and this may all be part of my wild imagination, but I do have distinct feeling that maybe this should have been left u…"

5. The Pursuit

It was now 1905 and this horror was upon the little town of Bowral, and as Cooling's story made its way through town there was a common uprising of courage through fear. This all erupted on the Friday night, a night when they knew there would be another gathering at the Green's farm. That night the faithful town folk congregated in the church. Among them was Steve Cooling, with the Reverend handing down the marching orders for the lynch mob that would rid this town of the evil of Mr Green and Charlene.

They left the church with weapons, home-made adaptations borne from the tools of their trade, but weapons nonetheless. They made their way through the town and to the Green farm where they witnessed from the bushes the wild orgy inside the house. They could see through the few windows the naked bodies drinking the foul beverage made from the mushrooms in the farm, and the drunkenly sexual motions that followed. But they could not see Mr Green or Charlene. They decided to wait until the two leaders could be seen before they made their attack; their plans, however, were foiled.

From the large stable, two caravans led by horses trotted out and the party inside the house came to a close. The men and women in the house began to dress themselves and walked out to the caravans. Within a space of under five minutes the house was deserted and the caravans were filled with the members of the gathering. Mr Green and Charlene were each leading one caravan. When the caravans were full they gave the horses a gentle whip and began the migration out of the farm.

The lynch mob stood in the bushes amazed at the sight they had just seen—there was nothing left for them to do. The evil they wanted to banish was leaving on its own accord. But the Reverend was not satisfied; he rightly pointed out that evil had no boundaries and they had to finish God's work, meaning to follow the caravans and kill the inhabitants at the first chance. Some of the men in the lynch mob were a little reluctant to follow, and they headed back home safely, knowing that evil had left their town. A small group of ten remained, armed and determined to bear the responsibility of ridding the world of this evil.

They followed the caravans through the night, keeping a manageable distance to avoid detection through the semi paths of the forest. This part of the forest hadn't been seen by most of the town folk as there had never been a need to venture so deep before, but the caravans pushed on with purpose to an undisclosed destination. Steve Cooling was among the "Faithful Few", as they were later referred to by the town folk. As they were traipsing through the bush he couldn't help but remember the story the doctor had recited, in particular the shadows that led Charlene to the professor's house. He wondered whether beyond the caravans there were shadows leading them, but he dared not look; instead he mentioned it to the Reverend. The

Reverend gripped his crucifix as he slowly made his way to the front of the lynch mob and raised his head up and above the bush to see if there was indeed anything leading the caravans. He froze in his tracks.

The lynch mob all stopped behind the Reverend as he crouched down, his face of fear was enough for the Faithful Few to know what he had seen. They all took stock of their courage and faith in their God and continued on as brave knights of the cross. The group stepped through rough terrain, keeping off any discernable path to maintain their secret pursuit.

Their best attempt at staying under this cloak of invisibility was fraught, however. Steve Cooling was first to hear a noise in the bushes past the trees they had just passed. The mob stopped in their tracks and turned to the source of the sound, trying to see through the darkness at what lurked past the trees. They didn't make a sound; deep down they didn't want to confront whatever crept behind the trees.

But their hopes fell on unforgiving fate, as the thick brush and trees parted with a gust of wind and the black shadowy cloud emerged and hovered above. The serpent shadow looked down upon the lynch mob for a moment, before swooping down and slithering through the men. Each man who met with the shadow fell to their knees in great pain before collapsing to the ground, their hearts failing them. Steve Cooling witnessed everything, but the serpent didn't attack him, only the eight other men, and it left as quickly as it had arrived.

Steve Cooling looked down at the mob, the dead men, whose lives were so easily taken by this dark force. Only he and Reverend remained. Steve's resolve was starting to shake, but the Reverend was quick to his aid, gripping his hand and quoting biblical phrases of courage. Steve and the Reverend decide to push on, their fate was certain in their minds, but if they retreated, they would not be honouring the lives of the eight men who lay before them.

The rest of the journey was not so long, only a few hundred metres, and they reached a small clearing where the caravans stopped. As Steve Cooling and the Reverend got closer they were amazed at the sight of a large house in the middle of the clearing and to the left, a church. The way the cult were leaving the caravans and entering this new house it would appear as though this house was built for them. A few short minutes passed before everyone was in the house and the doors were closed.

6. Birth of a town

Assessing the large house, and the absence of the serpent shadow, the two men felt their confidence return. They investigated all the routes to the house and the possible scenarios, especially given that there was now only two of them. Their plan was to set fire to the house; Steve Cooling had matches and all they needed was some loose dry shrub to put at the base of the house to ignite the fire. The Reverend and Steve set to work and before long they had amassed two small mountains of dead wood, leaves and debris at the front door of the house. Luckily the cult inside the house was so distracted by whatever ceremony they were holding that the two men's activities went unnoticed.

The Reverend, gripping his cross, whispered a prayer, and Steve Cooling lit the fire with his matches. On first attempt both stacks of kindle took the flame and immediately burst up along the wooden panels of the house, forcing Steve and the Reverend to take a step back. Both men gradually walked backwards as the flames grew higher and higher, their plan perfectly executed. Inside, meanwhile, they were still oblivious to flames outside the door and they carried on with their ceremony.

Steve Cooling and the Reverend stood by watching the flames climb up the front of the wooden building. As if there was some kind of external influence, the flames climbed higher at an incredible speed. But suddenly both men felt a force passing through them, and then they saw the dark shadow of the serpent pass through and towards the building. As fast as the flames grew and engulfed the building, the flames disappeared back to the small shrubs on the ground. The two men were stunned that they were still alive after coming in contact with the serpent shadow. But worse: Charlene and Mr Green emerged from the house.

Charlene floated towards Steve Cooling; both men were rooted to the ground, unable to move, either through fear or some kind of pressure holding them there. She whispered quietly into Steve's ear and floated back into the house, followed by Mr Green.

"What did she say, Steve?" the Reverend quickly asked.

Steve lifted his head, and tightened his grip on the heavy log of wood in his hand. "She said you need to die," Steve responded with a calm and dead look in his eyes.

With that Steve swung the wood and connected with the side of the Reverend's head. The Reverend was surprised by the attack and had little time to defend or ready himself for the impact. He was knocked to the ground, with blood trickling out from the gash on his temple.

When the Reverend woke up he was in the church, surrounded by the damned misfits of the cult, and at his feet stood Mr Green and Charlene. He tried to move, but his arms and legs were tied and bound to large steel hooks protruding from the floor. Looking beyond the crowd he saw five grotesque statues arranged in a circle, but apart from the unnatural appearance, he noticed each one had either a hole or something missing from the structure. But his analysis of the statues was interrupted as Steve emerged from the crowd and stood between Charlene and Mr Green with a large knife in hand.

Charlene laid her hand on Steve's back and ushered him towards the Reverend. Steve kneeled by his side, as Charlene spoke to the cult.

"We praise our god, Ahriman, for providing this town and the Reverend to complete our church and homage to our protectors. By his wisdom we have been led here, and by his minions' protection we will stay here and build a world dedicated to his will."

The Reverend meanwhile was having a myriad of thoughts running through his head, trying to look for ways he could escape. He knew what his fate would be, but wasn't sure his God and devotion would secure his escape. He thought, maybe this was his sacrifice to the world. He was chosen by his God, and his death would not be in vain and would lead to this dastardly cult being found out and ridden from this world.

Even with his religious rationale, his deepest instincts of fear and anger were still struggling to listen to his reason.

"What are you going to do with me, you whore?" The Reverend finally broke his silence.

Charlene smiled, not taking any offence at the Reverend's words, as she was beyond such trivial insults.

"Reverend, you have been chosen by Ahriman, as was Steve Cooling. You two will seal the future of our town, community and our immortality. You will be a part of us forever."

"What the hell do you mean? You've bewitched Steve, and you're going to sacrifice me to some heathen god…"

But before the Reverend could continue his theory, Charlene took a few steps forward and interrupted him.

"Yes, you will be sacrificed, but not in vain. You see, our protectors in this church need life, and you will provide that." She walked over to each statue as she explained the ghastly plans for the Reverend; first the goat, then the dragon, followed by the bull, the bat and finally the serpent.

"Our spirit protector will need your heart. Our fire protector will need your lungs. Our earth protector will need your torso. Our air protector will need your arms, and finally, Reverend, our water protector, which I'm sure you are familiar with by now, will need your mind. You see, you are so very important to us, Reverend, much more than you may think…"

"You can't do that. I will not give my soul. I am a man of God, the God that you will bow down to when…argh!"

The Reverend's protest was short lived, and ended when Steve thrust the knife into the Reverend's chest and a small amount of blood gargled in the Reverend's throat.

Charlene chuckled, along with Mr Green, at the man's feeble attempt at threatening them. Mr Green stepped over to Steve and whispered in his ear, instructing him further, and then turned to the Reverend.

"Poor Reverend Larwock, we don't want your soul. That's worthless to us, we just need your body. Your soul is tainted by the false god you worshipped and devoted yourself to. Steve, on the other hand, is pure of your depraved way of life. He is one of us now."

Steve's face and eyes remained unchanged, no emotion, his actions were not his own, gripping the knife handle again with further purpose. He watched the Reverend fade away and his eyes slowly lose their lively gaze.

Steve proceeded to cut open the Reverend's chest, breaking the rib cage open, revealing his heart and lungs. Charlene stepped towards the corpse of the Reverend and reached into his chest cavity and ripped out the lungs and heart and handed them out. The members handed them down the line to Mr Green as he placed them into the statues, where they would be stitched in.

Steve finally drove the knife into the Reverend's throat; the blood gushed and sprayed up onto Steve's face.

A book is found

Nomads from northern India made their way to Europe and southern Spain in the early fifteenth century. That group was the first of the nomads that the Europeans would call gypsies; riding through the lands in caravans with rumours of evil and misfortune following them. The locals never liked to see the gypsy caravans rolling into their towns and villages. They were afraid of that which they did not know, and gypsies represented a people with ideals that were alien to them. They had no permanent home and they carried knowledge that threatened the locals' way of life.

It was in such a town that adventurers and scholars Benjamin and James Everette stumbled upon a group of travellers who had stationed themselves on the outskirts of Malaga, a flourishing city in the south of Spain. The brothers were taking a week to recover from their recent travels and stocking up on supplies before moving north. Their aim was to make their way north-east to Seville, and settle there in the other thriving Spanish city.

But how Benjamin and James came to know this group was a product of survival, more than seeking friendship. Benjamin and James were in the area investigating some spectacular witchcraft allegations that had been all but ignored by the Spanish authorities. In Spain, the main focus, which would later lead to the trials in Basque, were in northern Spain, not the south.

When they arrived in the adjoining town of Malaga, they were not met by the welcome they had hoped. In fact the Arabs that ruled Malaga were not forthcoming to Christian visitors. Tensions between the two religions were at a high, just prior to Christian rule in the late 1400s.

It all erupted on one night when James was caught taking a keen eye on one of the town elder's daughters. His casual glance was taken as a lustful one and the men beat him in that house and both Benjamin and James were summarily driven out of town.

They took refuge in a little clearing, with Benjamin attending to his brother's wounds. There, a young lady from behind the trees approached the couple. She spoke some Spanish, as did Benjamin, and they conversed shortly as Benjamin explained the situation. She hurriedly ushered them to their campsite, offering them medical assistance and a tent to stay in for the night.

That night, as James slept early to recover from his severe beating, Benjamin sat in the next tent sharing dinner with the elder of the clan. He spoke Indian, which Benjamin had a conversational knowledge of. He deduced that the group was of Persian descent, which had escaped, like many, to northern India once the Islamic conquest took Persia. They had maintained the Zoroastrian heritage and still partook in the rituals of the old religion.

Whilst in conversation, Benjamin could not help but notice a small wooden box that sat in the corner of the tent with a disproportionate lock on it. After a short while Benjamin asked the elder about the box, and why such an elaborate lock was used. The answer was not expected as the elder elaborated.

"Inside this box, my friend, is an evil book, taken by my forefathers out of our homeland. We have sworn to protect the world from its contents and those who would use it against the good people of the world. That is all you need to know about it," he said sternly.

Given the tone of the answer, Benjamin didn't feel that he needed to question it any further. He put it down to more superstitious nonsense that some people still maintained. Benjamin was a man of science and mathematics, with little tolerance for such musings. They finished dinner and the pleasant conversation and he returned to his tent for a restful sleep.

The next day was a different story. Benjamin woke to the edge of a sword against his throat. He flinched with fear as he opened his eye to the sight of the elder at his throat. That flinch was enough for the sharp edge of the sword to make a razor sharp cut on his throat, drawing a drop of blood. He stopped and in shock asked for an explanation.

The sum of it was that the book was missing, as was his brother James. Benjamin had no idea what to make of the mystery or how this was going to be resolved with his life intact.

"I am as mystified as you are, as to my brother's disappearance," Benjamin exclaimed.

"Your brother's presence is of less concern, compared to the dangers he will encounter in that book. If he has stolen the book to make a pact, I fear we will have no choice but to destroy him." The reply from the elder was heartless and firm.

"I will go with you, let me help you find him. I will retrieve the book for you, please, let me talk to him and end this ordeal peacefully," Benjamin pleaded with the elder.

"Very well, you will join us, but we will decide on your brother, if he remains sane of mind," the elder responded.

With that they quickly got a group together and set out to find his brother. They split into teams of three with the elder and his son accompanying Benjamin on their trek east, towards Malaga.

Approximately an hour passed as the three men made their way through the path in the forest, before coming to the same clearing that the brothers had retreated to the night before. There they found James, or whom they thought was James. Benjamin laid eyes on his brother, but for all intents and purposes it could have been a stranger. James had completely healed, but his eyes, tongue and intentions were definitely not his own.

James stood in the clearing, oblivious to the presence of of the three men, deeply focused on the book, which he had opened. The elder looked upon the renewed man with anger and fear, whilst his son was retreating in fear of the evil presence he felt. Benjamin was at a loss for words as he cautiously called out to his brother.

"James. James?" Benjamin's tone was apologetically unthreatening.

The man who was previously James, whilst looking down at the book, flicked his hands at the men, as if shooing a fly, motioning them to leave him. The elder, however, had a duty to fulfill and would not be denied his responsibilities. He mustered up his strength and took aim with his sword and ran at James. Benjamin had no time to stop him but he yelled out at the hasty aggression of the elder.

"STOP! No…"

But Benjamin's fear for his brother was soon calmed as James turned to the old man and opened his mouth wide.

He appeared to scream but there was no noise; in its place a black mist emitted from his mouth, and engulfed the elder. The man collapsed to his knees and fell to the ground, motionless. The elder's son had seen enough, and instead of taking revenge he ran back towards the campsite.

Benjamin stood still with fear, alone with a man that resembled his brother, but was definitely under an outside influence. Benjamin was an educated man, and one of a few people who wholly believed in science. Although he would pay lip service to the powers that be, that he still believed in the all mighty God, deep down he put all of it down to superstition and weak-minded people. But this was a complete revelation, and unless his brother had become an illusionist overnight, Benjamin had no explanation for what he was seeing. All he did know, was this was evil and everything he thought he knew was no more.

When James brought his brother Benjamin back to London a month later, he had no choice but to commit him to an asylum for mental evaluation. The staff and doctors at the asylum had seen this kind of behaviour before, and put it down to an infestation of some kind of legion that had impacted his mind.

After a few courses of leeches proved to be ineffective in treating this infection, Benjamin was put in a cell for his own protection. Caged like a prisoner, his madness would become increasingly worse.

The guards in the ward would often sit outside his cell, unbeknown to him, and listen to his wild stories as a form of amusement. Although some could not help the fear creeping into their bones as Benjamin would tell horrifying tales.

The guards would tell each other about these night-marish tales and would pass on these mad stories, about a man who could command a serpent-shaped black mist. He would take lives and destroy towns, commanding demons to do his bidding throughout southern Spain.

Although the events in the Malaga area proved to be true, the staff put it down to his madness finding some real events to hang stories on to convince him of the truth. But the claims were ridiculous in nature, especially his recantation of the death of a group of gypsies.

He recalled the story every night in fact. The group of gypsies was moving in haste to escape their fate from the mystical man. The possessed man, who only wanted evil, finally tracked them down and drew upon demons of the underworld, under the influence of the Zoroastrian evil god, Ahriman. He had the members of the travelling group stripped of their clothes and with his will hung their bodies from the trees, using the tree vines as nooses and skinning their bodies with a sword he had found. Their skin was burnt and their fat was consumed in liquid form to fortify his allegiance to his god and commit his descendants to the service of evil.

The way back

1. Unexplained phone call

He put the phone down on the bed side table, agitated and confused at the same time. Not only had the call come too early in the morning for him, but the claim the woman made was unexpected and not welcome. Stewart thought about returning to sleep, he still had another two hours before he had to ready himself to teach the first class of the day, Applied Mathematics 101 at Sydney University, a subject he wasn't looking forward to this term. But the phone call had woken him to the point where it was useless to return to bed. So he headed to the shower and took his time with his morning routine.

Looking into his bowl of cereal, he couldn't stop wondering whether there was any truth to the woman's claim, or if it was part of some kind of psychotic prank. But why prank him? His father wasn't anybody special. The news of his disappearance didn't really raise any alarms for the authorities and only brought sadness to the few family members and friends. He checked his phone again, looking through the calls that had been made to him, and he found her phone number. His hand hovered over the number, wanting to call, but not, all at the same time. He took another milk-filled scoop of his cereal, and pressed the call button.

"Hi, is this Stewart?" the voice on the other end answered, but Stewart was not so fast to respond.

He had hoped that she wouldn't know it was him, at least not until he had time to talk first and feel out the conversation, but now she was in control.

"Yes, I…" he sheepishly responded.

He was cut off, a tone of excitement came from the woman's voice on the phone, grateful that her call was returned and not ignored.

"I'm so glad you called back. Before I tell you anything, I want you to know that I am sorry for your loss, and I'm not doing this to bring back sad memories, I just want to tell you the truth, and if you want we can find his murderers." She rattled through the introduction as if it had been rehearsed a few times.

"Murderers? He wasn't killed! He died because he was lost in the woods," Stewart shot back.

He was convinced as were the police about the demise of his father 25 years ago. His father's body was never found, but his car was found driven off the edge of the road some fifteen kilometres west of Bowral, a tourist town in the south west of Sydney. The forest in that area was thick and unforgiving, for a man with no skill in surviving, and after sustaining injuries from the accident it was a foregone conclusion that he had died there. Some clothes were recovered near the river, which led to the conclusion that his body was swept away in the river. By police estimations, they had started the search approximately three weeks after the accident, which was long enough to cease the search and investigation.

"Look, I've been researching this case for about five years now, and I am absolutely sure I know what happened. Can we meet today to talk about this over coffee? I don't want to do this over the phone." Her voice circled through his head, however, he was still in deep thought.

"Yes. I'll finish at two, why don't you meet me at Toby's Estate, the café just off Broadway?" he finally responded.

The woman agreed and hung up, leaving Stewart to go even further into thought about what this could mean. He was not sure if he believed her; his curiosity, however, was too strong to ignore.

After his class, Stewart wasted no time in leaving the university and making his way to the coffee shop for the rendezvous he had been looking forward to for the last few hours. He stepped into the café, suddenly realising that he had no idea what she looked like, so he called her again, and to his surprise a young strawberry blonde-haired woman in the corner answered her phone. She was attractive without being glamorous, but Stewart was still quite taken by her appearance, which helped her cause.

"I'm so glad you made it, I was thinking you wouldn't come." She had a genuinely grateful voice.

They sat down at the table, but there was an awkward silence, neither knowing how to begin the conversation, until Stewart broke the silence.

"So tell me what you know, Shannon," he said.

Shannon began to reveal the findings of her investigations, with supporting documents and newspaper clippings.

"Okay, you will need you to hear me out on this, because some of it may sound a little strange. Firstly, your father wasn't lost, he was kidnapped and murdered. To understand what happened I have to tell you the full story, which goes back about almost 200 years. You realise, Stewart, you're the first person that's going to hear me telling this story? I wouldn't dare tell anyone—people would think I'd gone crazy."

Stewart eased her vulnerability with a comforting smile, so she continued with the excitement of a young child telling her parents about her day at school.

2. The story of the father

"Stewart, there is a town that exists near Bowral, which is not on the map and can only be found once every 25 years. I know how that sounds, but I'm being serious; this town is under some kind of spell, which began about 200 years ago. Back then there was a group of witches who left Bowral and settled in this town, which remains invisible to the rest of the world.

"Now, the link to you and your father is that the leader of the group of witches was a Mr Green. I couldn't find his first name; your father was a descendent of that family."

"Wait, how do you even know that? As far as I know we've never had a Green, our surname is Diamine," Stewart was quick to interrupt.

"Yes I know, but what you don't know, and what your father didn't know was that his mother's maiden name was Green," Shannon replied. There was a pause, as Shannon allowed Stewart to accept the fact before following on.

"From what I can gather, every 25 years, someone in that blood line somehow finds their way into this town and disappears. I've done some other research and found pretty nasty stuff. There was a report that before this group of witches left Bowral, this red-haired woman called Charlene Everett came to town. She was known to hold some ancient Persian magic book. What I figure, which I think fits with the story, they sacrifice a descendent of Mr Green to appease their gods and so they can continue living in this invisible town."

She took a break to take sip of her coffee. Stewart took that moment to digest what he had just heard. There were too many loose ends for his liking.

"Wait there. You have to admit this is all a bit far-fetched, but ignoring that part, let's analyse this story. What's the name of the town?"

Silence followed; Shannon didn't know the name of the town, only descriptions and fables about a mysterious place.

"Okay, fine, how are these people still alive? You said they settled there 200 years ago, and no one goes in or out except for one of these descendants. I mean it's a bit incestuous…" Stewart's tone took on that of a professional investigative journalist, grilling a politician on prime time TV.

"No, you don't get it—the sacrifice is for their immortality. The people there are the same people that settled there. According to this book of magic, the leader had to sacrifice his body to the group for them to stay there and to be immortal, and his soul would ascend." She was confident in her story.

"So they kill someone every 25 years and…" Stewart was interrupted again with more of a grim reality.

"They don't just kill; they eat the descendant. It's a cannibalistic ritual!" she shot back.

This seemed to be reaching the limit of Stewart's tolerance, and with an apologetic smile he stood up. "I'm sorry, Shannon, but I've heard enough. I think it's best I leave now and we forget this conversation…"

"Please don't leave Stewart. I'm trying to help you, you could be next." Shannon's voice carried over the café and Stewart paused.

Shannon saw her opportunity. "Tamara…she will take you there."

This final comment seemed to resonate with Stewart on some level and he turned back and sat back down at the table.

"Okay, tell me everything you know." He seemed much more interested now.

This was Shannon's hook and she explained to Stewart that her father left his mother at an early age because of a girl named Tamara. She was the reason that his father had left the family, and she was the one that brought the male descendants to the town.

Shannon then put to Stewart her plan for finding and ending this abomination. A plan that involved taking Stewart to the town, much like Tamara would, but at least he would know what's waiting and they would be able to stop it.

Stewart had little confidence in any plan. He did pose two questions: firstly, how they would enter the town; and secondly, how were they going to destroy the town and its people?

Shannon had an answer only for the second question. "When we are in the town, we will have to destroy the statues in the church. If what I've read is true and this is what they've done, then there will be five statues in the church, each one containing a body part or organ of a holy man. We will need to decapitate the one that's got the head of the holy man.

"Depending on what demons they've decided to choose as their protectors, one of them will be the dominant one and that's the one we need to decapitate. If we can do that, then we undo the creation of the town and its people."

"Undo?" Stewart responded. He found the choice of words interesting to say the least.

Shannon, however, had taken time to read and study the material and her use of the word was quite deliberate.

"Yes, we are not going there to blow up the town and kill its people. What we will do is destroy that town and everyone in it will vanish from human history as if it never existed." There was definite malice to her tone and resolve.

Stewart took a moment to digest Shannon's entire story; to him it was so far a very fantastical tale.

Shannon had hoped that she had convinced him of the truth, which to her was absolute. To her dismay, however, Stewart was not convinced.

He was not going to continue the conversation or take any action on such a speculative theory. He had to admit he was intrigued by the story, as would anyone, but it was not enough for him to join what he suspected was a somewhat mentally instable woman, whose research had gone off a tangent into the realms of madness.

Shannon tried to plead with Stewart, but she noticed that she had lost him, and avoiding the risk of appearing insane she sat back and sighed in defeat. She watched Stewart leave; all her research over the last few years may have been wasted if Stewart didn't go along with her plan. Her hopes weren't all dashed, however. Before Stewart had left the café, his phone rang.

"Hi Tammy, yeah, just finishing up, I'll see you soon…"

That was enough for Shannon, but this meant that she had to watch over him. They were already in contact with Stewart, which meant his sacrifice was imminent.

3. Night before the road trip

That night Stewart had a hard time getting to sleep, the disturbing story that he had heard earlier in the day was still swirling around his head like a threatening snake ready to strike. He decided he needed to reset his mind, so he left the bed and entered the living room to kill some time watching TV. Moments later his girlfriend entered the room, sleepy and dressed in a singlet and pyjama pants covering her tall slender body. A sweet face with perfectly proportioned features and long brown straight hair with a princess part. She approached Stewart on the sofa and sat next to him, cuddling his arm and laying her head on his shoulder.

"What's wrong baby?" she said in a tender tone.

"Nothing, just got a lot on my mind," Stewart said as he lovingly looked at her and caressed her face.

"Not that I want to add more stress, but can we visit my parents this weekend?" She sat back apologetically as the words rolled off her tongue.

"Tammy, really? You want to tell me now? It's such short notice."

She inched her way forward and back on his shoulder, willing her warmth onto his body.

"I know. Mum and I have been talking about it, and she said this weekend would be best for them. We can leave in the morning and be in Bowral by about eleven. Just in time for lunch." She flashed her pleading smile to convince him.

Stewart uninterestingly nodded, and got a kiss for his troubles as Tammy went back to bed with a spring in her step.

As he sat there numbingly watching the TV, he realised that the story Shannon had told him earlier in the day was getting a little too close to reality. Not only was his girlfriend's name Tamara, but her parents that he had never met lived in Bowral and she suddenly wanted to go visit them with very little notice.

He tried to dismiss it as an accidental correlation, but something deep down was troubling him and bringing up all kinds of questions in his mind. Either this was a coincidence, or what Shannon was telling him was rooted in some sort of truth. But what if there were a sick group of people living in the forest who believed all of this, and went through with sacrificial rituals, killing innocent people; and Tamara was the one who wooed innocent men to their final fate?

Meanwhile, Shannon was sitting outside in her car watching over Stewart's apartment from the street. She witnessed the exchange that took place, but only noticed the shadows that were walking from one room to another. She decided that she would sleep in the car that night and made herself comfortable. But no sooner had she put her head back that she noticed something strange. The female shadow floated back into the room, then the shadow seemed to turn to the window and the edges of the shadow became less defined.

Moments later the shadow turned into a dark mist in the shape of a serpent. Shannon sank back in her seat; she felt the shadow was looking directly at her, but she dared not move or make a sound.

Shannon couldn't control a short whimper as the shadow penetrated the window and flew outside, slowly but directly towards her. She fumbled her keys, but they fell out of her hand and to the floor. She bent over to find the keys and knocked her forehead into the steering wheel so hard that she opened a gash.

She sat back up only to notice the black shadow was now at her car and seeping into her car through the window and floor of the car. The fear and the presence of this being sent Shannon into hyperventilation; her breathing became faster and louder and deeper, she had lost all control. Her brain was in overdrive trying to work out an escape, trying to control her breathing, trying to keep her alive.

Shannon woke up with the morning sun beating through the windscreen and onto her face. She blinked a few times adjusting to the light, then wiped her hands over her eyes, but there was a strange sensation under her hands, a thick sludgy wetness. She quickly looked at the palm of her hands, crimson hands, her face was covered in blood. She screamed for a moment. Then frantically she felt her forehead, thinking that the dream may have been real, but she felt no pain or irregularities on her skin. She reached into her glove box and retrieved a pack of wet tissues and proceeded to clean her face to reveal no scars, just blood.

She knew now what she had been investigating was very real and she too was involved and had no choice but to continue her path. They knew she existed and what her plans were, and they would not let her walk away or continue her life as before. Upon this revelation, she looked over at Stewart's apartment, but the scene on the street was more interesting. Stewart had a travel bag in hand and was putting it in the boot of his car. Meanwhile, a slender brown-haired woman approached the car, kissing Stewart on the cheek before sitting down in the passenger's seat. Once Stewart had finished loading the car, the couple made their way down the street. The road trip had begun, and Shannon would have to follow them if she was going to complete her mission.

4. Alliances found

Shannon muttered to herself as she drove her car, reciting the plan in her mind until it was solid and foolproof, all the while keeping one eye on the car that was within her view. Stewart's car was maybe ten to fifteen car lengths ahead, driven in the southern direction towards the town and maybe to his final fate. Shannon was determined to correct this evil in the world, and this was her only chance to rid the world of this black dot that had sullied its history. After being confronted by the black shadowy mist that came to her car in the dream and the blood on her face, she knew that this could take her life too.

Just past the exit at Wollongong there was something peculiar ahead, a murder of black crows, not a sight that's naturally seen or witnessed regularly. She noticed this queer flock gather and hover over Stewart's car; like a cloud the crows cast a shadow under which Stewart drove unknowingly. This continued for a few minutes before three of the murder flew away from the congregation and circled back and out of view.

This sight would not have drawn any attention, and indeed, other motorists probably didn't notice this, but Shannon was acutely aware of the world beyond her own. Her thoughts were interrupted though as she spotted the three crows flying down towards her car. Shockingly they were not slowing down or changing their direction; Shannon clenched her teeth and tightened her grip on the steering wheel.

A moment later the three crows in unison smashed down onto the windshield of her car with a loud thud. She swerved on impact, losing control of the car momentarily, crossing lanes and almost crashing into other cars. She screamed as she slammed her foot on the brake and the car came to a sudden stop.

The birds were all dead, one still on her car, their blood obscuring her view, but she was safe. She had instinctively pulled into the hard shoulder and out of harm's way. However, Stewart's car was now beyond view and she was at a loss at how she would pick up his trail.

She sat in the car, defeated, trying to rehash the plan that had now been severely shattered, but there was no bright spark of inspiration in her mind. The best alternative she conjured up was that if she continued to Bowral, there may be another way to the mysterious town on foot. With somewhat renewed energy and resolve she let the windscreen wipers remove the blood and carcass from her windscreen and she drove to Bowral.

Upon arriving in the historic town of Bowral, Shannon quickly found the local library, as she was convinced there might be some information buried in the town records. What she needed was access to local town newspapers and notices from mid-1905, but for some reason that whole year was missing from the chronological list of records. This was a either a mistake, or a deliberate attempt to hide the dark past of the town. In any case, Shannon had no time to question the motives, she needed those missing newspapers.

The librarian was a lady in her fifties, stern and weathered, with long grey hair tied up in a tight ponytail. She gazed menacingly with her aged green eyes at Shannon as she was asked about the missing records. She knew Shannon had other motives besides research.

"Why do you want records from that year?" she asked accusingly.

Shannon started out being apologetic, thinking that a sympathetic approach may help her cause.

"It's the final piece of my report on Bowral, and that's the one year I couldn't find anything about, which is why I drove all the way here…I was hoping that the library of Bowral would be the best source for that information."

The librarian was suspicious, but strangely trusting of Shannon's motives. She could not place it, but she felt a connection with Shannon, so she agreed.

The librarian motioned to Shannon and they walked to the back corner of the library, to a wooden door. Upon entering the room of physical records, the librarian turned back to Shannon.

"Am I correct in saying you are on our side?"

Shannon was caught by surprise, and she stumbled over her positive response, not quite knowing where the line of questioning would lead to. She wasn't at all comfortable in this dimly lit room alone with the librarian. The librarian, however, looked pleased with the answer.

"I thought so. If you are looking for that year, then you know what you're looking for, and you know that it's happening again tomorrow…"

Shannon's eyes lit up with fear. "Wait…tomorrow? That's too early…I need to save him…"

The librarian was even more intrigued by her comment and waited for Shannon to elaborate, and was told the full story and of her following Stewart to Bowral. The librarian took Shannon to the far end of the records room and opened a small wooden cupboard door revealing a large knife hanging above a glass of water.

"You're the only person that's seen this. But I feel that you and I were destined to meet on a day like today, and under such circumstances. It's not too late, and this dagger will be the instrument we need to end Larwock."

Shannon reached out to touch the knife but the librarian blocked her progress and closed the cupboard door, locking it again.

"Who are you?" Shannon finally asked the librarian.

The librarian didn't answer; instead she took Shannon to the table and chair in the middle of the room. On the table there was a large book and a lamp overhead, which she turned on. Shannon peered down at the book; the writing was in a strange language, each letter or word made up of horizontal and vertical lines. She had a feeling she knew what the book was, but wanted to know for sure.

"Is this the Book of Ahriman?" she asked.

With the lamp illuminating her face beyond the dim light around her, the librarian finally revealed her identity.

"My name is Amanda Larwock. I'm the great granddaughter of Reverend Larwock, who served in Bowral. He was the leader of the 'Faithful Few' who banished that obscene cult from Bowral.

"But what he didn't know was that he was the chosen holy man that was needed to secure that god forsaken town. This book, yes, you are right, it's the book of Ahriman. I've been studying this book my whole life. It was passed down to me by my mother, and before that my grandfather, who was the first to discover the book when he tried to destroy that town.

"You have to realise, this town that is my namesake, the extermination of it is my family's purpose. I know how to find Larwock through the forest and unlock the gates, and I have the instrument to extinguish the fire that keeps that town alive."

5. The way to Larwock

The sun was setting on the town of Bowral, but inside the records room of the library, Amanda and Shannon were only beginning their fatal adventure. They were not packing anything except for courage and knowledge of what was ahead of them on that foul night. Amanda, however, had one item to take, and she opened the cupboard to the dagger. She took a moment to think, then finally turned to Shannon.

"You should take this dagger, Shannon. When the time comes, you will be responsible for extinguishing the fire and destroying the statue bearing my ancestor's head."

Shannon was surprised and wary of taking on the responsibility. She hesitated at first, but then reached out to grip the knife. Amanda again blocked her hand.

"Not so hasty, Shannon, that knife will burn your hand. The first person to grip it will be its owner. When you hold it, know that it will burn, but only as long as it takes you to pour the glass of water over your hand. Do you understand?"

Shannon was a little dubious of the claim, but she honoured Amanda's instructions, and sure enough as she gripped the knife she felt the burning pain on the palm of her hand, as if pressing her hand against a hot iron. She quickly poured the water over her hand and knife, and with the splash the pain subsided. Shannon inspected the knife and her hand and was astonished that her palm had no burns or blisters from the sharp heat of the dagger.

Later that night, Amanda and Shannon, with dagger in hand, made their way through the town in Shannon's car until they reached a dirt road leading to a local farm, an abandoned farm with the forest beyond it.

"This is the old Green farm. No one has lived here since that wretched group left Bowral, and the land itself is infertile and unholy. We need to drive to the edge of the forest and we will go on foot from there." Amanda had obviously been down this road before.

Shannon did as advised and they began the rest of the journey on foot through the forest. With no trail to guide them and the moonlight finding it difficult to break through, the journey became a gruelling one. The forest was quiet, very quiet, no noise besides their footsteps, which Shannon felt was strange given the wildlife in the area. Amanda was aware of the reasons; she had been through this area once before and knew the evil in the forest that protected the town. All wildlife in this forest had left long ago, the fear of the unknown and evil that lay near drove them out.

Before long they were at a small clearing. Amanda stopped to assess her surroundings, taking her time to pick the right direction, but Shannon noticed something in the woods.

"Amanda, there's something out there," Shannon said in the quietest of whispers.

Amanda, however, was looking in the opposite direction, where there was something ghastly already in sight.

Shannon turned her gaze towards it and was immediately hit with a stench that almost triggered her reflux. The vision, however, was enough to disrupt her vomit. The grave image she witnessed was of an goat-shaped black mist with glowing white eyes floating towards them. Shannon started to tremble as she turned back to where she heard the first noise, and there she found another misty creature, a black bull whose horns extended up, forming a white burning fire.

Amanda quickly pushed Shannon to the ground and ordered her to close her eyes and not open them until she instructed. Shannon felt the stench even more heavy in the air and the heat of the fire was starting to burn her skin, but she didn't flinch and she kept her eyes closed.

Just then she heard Amanda muttering some words, her voice became louder and louder as she progressed as if growing in strength and confidence. The words were foreign, but she heard parts of it as Amanda's voice started to boom through the air. Her voice peaked, with a volume and an echo unnatural for a human voice, repeating the chant over and over again

"Kê verethrem-jâ thwâ pôi sêñghâ ýôi heñtî cithrâ môi dãm ahûmbish ratûm cizhdî at hôi vohû seraoshó jañtû manranghâ mazdâ ahmâi ýahmâi vashî kahmâicît…

"Kê verethrem-jâ thwâ pôi sêñghâ ýôi heñtî cithrâ môi dãm ahûmbish ratûm cizhdî at hôi vohû seraoshó jañtû manranghâ mazdâ ahmâi ýahmâi vashî kahmâicît…

"Kê verethrem-jâ thwâ pôi sêñghâ ýôi heñtî cithrâ môi dãm ahûmbish ratûm cizhdî at hôi vohû seraoshó jañtû manranghâ mazdâ ahmâi ýahmâi vashî kahmâicît!!!"

Finally Shannon felt a cool breeze come through and

a strong all-encompassing light that she could see through her eyelids illuminated the dark night. As quickly as these came they also disappeared. Everything went quiet again and the dark returned before Shannon felt a soft hand on her shoulder.

"You can open your eyes, Shannon, it's quite safe now." Amanda's voice was reassuringly calming and her fear faded away as she opened her eyes.

Briefly, there was a weight off their shoulders as the over-bearing evil in the forest seemed to have disappeared, or at least subsided for the moment. The familiar feelings rushed back, however, when Amanda discovered the unholy gates to Larwock.

They walked towards a disguised wall covered in weeds and wall climbers, which they had not noticed moments before. But this wall was very real and tangible. The two started to peel off the weeds to reveal the stone behind it. There was a distinct line in the middle separating the two stones, but this was no door that could be opened by hand; this needed a key of some sort. Shannon looked lost, but Amanda knew what was needed.

"Shannon, I need you to cut my arm," Amanda said as she revealed her forearm.

She was sceptical but kept one eye closed as she pro-ceeded to lacerate Amanda's arm. The wound was on the vein and blood was in good supply as it pumped out her arm. Amanda stepped over to the gates; with her finger she retrieved blood from the open wound and began to write on the wall, in the same text as the book.

The ground began to tremble ever so slightly and small

amounts of rock started falling down and out of the slit of the gates. The sound of stone on stone grinding became louder as the gates began to dislodge from aeons of decay and reveal the town inside, along with a stench that ungrace-fully floated in the air.

6. Nothing

It was dusk when they entered Larwock through the stone gates. Shannon took a look back to the gates only to see the forest instead. The stone gates and night that lay beyond it back to Bowral had disappeared and were replaced by this new place. This was not a town near Bowral; this was a town that did not belong on earth. This confirmed everything she had read and researched over the last few years and the truth was now more unsettling than the fantasy of a place like this existing. But she suppressed her fear and discomfort for where her feet lay, she knew she had a responsibility to not only keep Stewart alive, but also to fulfill her task with the dagger.

The two made their way through the outskirts of the town to the main road, much like Reverend Larwock and Steve Coolings had when they rose up against the evil of this clan. They soon found the main road of the town. It was a quaint town, and harmless, with regular stores, but as the sun was setting there was a queerness in the air that made the town seem more sinister than it appeared. They spotted the Elder Inn, which was lit up inside, busy with people drinking and dancing. This affirmed Shannon's fears that they may have been too late to save Stewart, a feeling that Amanda seemed to share as well. They didn't hesitate as they made their way to the main road and walked towards the inn.

As they stepped into the middle of the road, a voice from behind stilted their progress.

"Can I help you, ladies?" a masculine voice said.

He approached them as he put his keys in his pocket. The man was just leaving the local café and locking up for the night. He was middle aged with a balding hair line and a dark beard covering his jaw line. He brandished a friendly smile and genuine helpful demeanour. Amanda didn't fall for the charm. She approached the man and seemed to over-power him by her will. He remained in the same position, unable to move or defend himself while Amanda placed her hand on his forehead and spoke in the ancient tongue.

"Yathâ ahû vairyô athâ ratush ashâtcît hacâ."

The man fell to his knees with his hands over his head writhing in pain. Shannon witnessed his hands ageing. In seconds the man looked like he had aged fifty years. His skin wrinkled and became limp, and his bones appeared more defined as the muscles started to waste away. He looked up with a face of anger and agony.

"YOU BITCH!" he cried.

But he didn't have the strength to stand or take action. Instead he slumped further down, ageing into death and beyond. His body decayed at lightning speed, till only large bones remained, and the rest turned to dust and sank into the ground.

Shannon was shocked at the transformation of the man into ruin, and looked back at Amanda, realising that Amanda was more than she let on. A great power dwelled inside her. Amanda felt Shannon's uneasy peace with what had transpired.

"Shannon, when I said I have studied the book, that's what I meant. I have learnt a great deal, some good, some bad. But nothing I learnt took me on the wrong path. The powers I use, I use against evil. What you just saw was a wicked man, a man that has killed and would kill again. There are no innocent people in this town…and that includes us."

The two turned their attention back on the Elder Inn; the party was somewhat subdued. Instead of drinking and dancing, through the windows they could see the hoard circling around the centre of the room. They slowly crept up to the window and peered inside. Their hearts sank as, in the middle of that room, Stewart lay helpless whilst a man with a knife, similar to Shannon's, began cutting his chest open. Shannon saw the looks on the faces of the group as their eyes turned ravenous and their mouths began to salivate at the sight of blood and freshly cut human flesh.

She was disgusted by the image and the absolute insanity that fuelled such a desire for cannibalism. Amanda motioned for Shannon towards the church.

"There is nothing we can do here, Shannon. You need to do the final bidding, whilst the coven is busy with their feast." Amanda had a sense of urgency in her voice.

But Shannon didn't want to be alone in her quest. "What about you?" Shannon quickly asked.

Amanda's answer didn't come, as the door of the Elder Inn opened before them. They both stood to their feet, as Charlene Everette stepped out. Long red hair framed her attractive face with baby white skin, and she was dressed in a flowing white cotton robe, stained with the fresh blood she had just consumed.

Amanda pushed Shannon away. Charlene was all too aware of the two women's reasons for being in Larwock.

"Yes, Shannon, you go to the church. Young Ms Larwock wants to redeem her family pride. Oh, Ms Larwock, your family will never learn." Charlene's tone was mocking and drunk with bloodlust.

Shannon didn't need any further invitation; she ran towards the church. Meanwhile Amanda stood her ground for an encounter she had prepared for her whole life. She stared deep into Charlene's eyes, and with complete focus she muttered the Zoroastrian prayers that would bring on the demise of the witch.

Charlene paused; this was not something she expected from the young Larwock woman. She felt great power exuding from Amanda's words, and it was something that she hadn't felt before.

"I'm glad you didn't come unprepared," Charlene said as she struggled forward.

Her next step fell short and she went down to one knee, as a sharp pain travelled through her abdomen. Where there was a mocking nature to her manner and voice was now replaced with a serious threat. Charlene struggled back to her feet, shouting at the top of her voice.

"ENOUGH!" Charlene's voice reverberated throughout the whole town.

Amanda's voice cracked and no sound emitted from her mouth. Her mind suddenly became a mess of words and languages with no logical progression.

Meanwhile, Shannon had reached the church, but was met with a surprise. An acute heat burnt her skin as she approached. She paused for a moment, and the truth revealed itself. Before her eyes, a wall of fire came into view, burning with hellish intensity. She thought for a moment; how was she to penetrate the flames, and still be alive to destroy the statues? This was not something that they had planned for.

Charlene's voice interrupted all her thoughts and she looked back at Amanda. It was a dire moment as Amanda gazed back at Shannon. Charlene held her by the neck and thrust a knife in her upper abdomen and began to force the knife up, cutting and breaking through rib cage all the way through her neck and up to her chin.

Shannon broke down, witnessing Amanda meeting such a devastating fate at the hands of Charlene. She was lost without her and had no idea how to fulfil her task. She fell to her knees, the weight of all the events of the last few days breaking her spirit. Meanwhile she could see Charlene make her way towards her, knowing she would meet the same fate.

But then, a strange vision behind Charlene, the man that had handed Charlene her knife stood locking his eyes with Shannon's. Not speaking but willing her to stand up. Then a voice travelled to her through the wind, breaking through the evil around it like a bright light in the darkest night.

"Save me, Shannon." The voice had power in it that lifted Shannon.

She stood up in time to confront Charlene, who was only a few feet away from her.

"Join us, Shannon." Charlene's words seemed to carry all the evil in the world, but it washed off Shannon's spirit.

"What will you do, Shannon? You realise you have reached your end. You don't know what you're doing." Charlene's mocking tone returned.

"I will cut the head off that statue in the church!" Shannon shouted back defiantly.

Charlene smiled like a mother smiling upon her child's claims to courageous actions.

"Shannon, you can't wield the power of that knife, only a Cooling…" Charlene paused for a moment.

She looked back at the inn and saw Steve Cooling standing outside, looking in on the events. It suddenly dawned on her. Shannon was a descendant of Steve Cooling. This was the day that she feared when the Faithful Few return to free their ancestors and destroy Larwock. Her face turned to terror and she felt Shannon growing in stature and power. Before she had a moment to take any action, Shannon thrust her dagger into the fire.

"No!" Charlene's once powerful voice seemed to have lost its thunder.

The flames subsided and parted to let Shannon through. She looked back and Charlene had dropped to her knees. Shannon quickly ran into the church, and was first hit with that horrible stench of rotting flesh, and now she had seen the source of the smell. The human flesh that was attached to these statues was rotten. She fought hard to compose herself and keep herself on track. She assessed each statue, one more grotesque than the other. Finally she arrived at the sea serpent, which had the head of Reverend Larwock. It had grotesquely taken on some of the serpent facial features and structure, and its resemblence to a human face was slowly disappearing. She knew this was the statue that had to be decapitated.

"STOP…!" Charlene ordered with one last gasp.

Charlene stepped through the furious fire, but her skin and hair burnt instantly, her skin glistened as multiple layers were burnt off revealing naked flesh. The pain was too great for her to step into the church. She pleadingly reached out to Shannon to stop, but Shannon was determined to carry out the task. She pierced the neck of the statue with the dagger and ripped off the head.

Charlene screamed as the head was removed, her voice echoed through the church and the town, followed by the collective screams of the coven still in the Elder Inn. The flames outside the church vanished into smoke, and with a snap everything turned to white.

Everything had dissolved into white. All the screams had quietened down to nothing. Shannon felt no air or ground and could not see beyond the infinite white. Then she realised she wasn't breathing or standing. She was suspended in nothingness. Shannon closed her eyes, hoping and praying that when she opened them again, everything would return to normal.

She waited a few moments and slowly opened her eyes.